Fabulous FATHERS

**He's more than a man
he's a fabulous father**

AVAILABLE JUNE 2009
1) *Anything for Danny* by Carla Cassidy
2) *Father in the Making* by Marie Ferrarella
3) *Most Wanted Dad* by Arlene James
4) *The Nine-Month Bride*
by Judy Christenberry

AVAILABLE AUGUST 2009
5) *Instant Father* by Lucy Gordon
6) *Daddy Lessons* by Stella Bagwell
7) *Most Eligible Dad* by Karen Rose Smith
8) *First Time, Forever* by Cara Colter

AVAILABLE SEPTEMBER 2009
9) *A Father's Promise* by Helen R. Myers
10) *The Women in Joe Sullivan's Life*
by Marie Ferrarella
11) *Falling for a Father of Four*
by Arlene James
12) *Caleb's Son* by Laurie Paige

AVAILABLE OCTOBER 2009
13) *Waiting for the Wedding* by Carla Cassidy
14) *Daniel's Daddy* by Stella Bagwell
15) *Always Daddy* by Karen Rose Smith
16) *The Billionaire's Baby Chase*
by Valerie Parv

Blaine O'Connor on Fatherhood...

Dear Mickey,

I guess you could say I became your father twice—once when you were born, and once when you turned ten and your mother died. Those first ten years, I was more your friend than your dad. I got to see you so rarely that I wanted to make the very most of those precious times we shared. I didn't want to mar those visits by telling you when to go to bed or to pick up your clothes. I just wanted to enjoy you and make you happy.

But suddenly you were mine, and I was your dad twenty-four hours a day. It became my responsibility to see to it that you grew up to be a fine young man. I don't mind telling you that I really had my doubts about handling the job so well.

It didn't help when your godmother came butting in, doing everything right, making me feel even more lost in this vast wonderland called fatherhood. But don't worry, Mickey— I'll figure this whole thing out. No bossy lady is going to tell me how to raise my kid. Who needs her, anyway?

From now on, it'll be just us guys. Won't that be great?

Love,

Dad

Fabulous
FATHERS

MARIE FERRARELLA
Father in the Making

Silhouette® Books

Published by Silhouette Books
America's Publisher of Contemporary Romance

 SILHOUETTE BOOKS

Recycling programs
for this product may
not exist in your area.

ISBN-13: 978-0-373-18886-4

FATHER IN THE MAKING

Copyright © 1995 by Marie Rydzynski-Ferrarella

Visit Silhouette Books at www.eHarlequin.com

Printed in U.S.A.

MARIE FERRARELLA

This *USA TODAY* bestselling and RITA® Award-winning author has written more than 150 novels for Silhouette Books, some under the name Marie Nicole. Her romances are beloved by fans worldwide. Visit her Web site at www.marieferrarella.com.

To Adrienne Macintosh and
brand-new relationships.

Chapter One

He had no idea how to be a father. The very thought brought a nervous ripple to his digestive tract, though his smile remained fixed for Mickey's benefit.

He knew all about being a friend. Over the years, he had pretty well perfected the part and derived a great deal of pleasure from it. As had Mickey. Mickey was all that mattered. He always had been.

But he hadn't a clue how to be a father. Though his son was now ten years old, until this week Blaine O'Connor had never had to don the sober, heavy robes of fatherhood.

They were thrust on him without ceremony, without a whisper of a warning. They were pushed upon him as suddenly as they had been pulled out of his hands eleven years ago.

Then he hadn't even been able to try them on for size. He'd found out sheerly by accident after the divorce papers had been filed that Diane was pregnant. Once he knew, Blaine had wanted to give the floundering marriage another try for the sake of the unborn child they had created. But Diane had refused to listen.

It gave her, he thought, a special sense of satisfaction to deny him that reconciliation. Almost as much satisfaction as when she refused to let him be present at his son's birth. He'd been robbed of the joy of seeing his only child come into the world.

All because Diane had had no idea what the word *trust* meant.

Angry, hurt, Diane had attempted to completely force him out of Mickey's world. Blaine hadn't been allowed to make any decisions affecting the boy. And so, he'd had no training as a father, not even a dress rehearsal.

Blaine stepped out of a moving man's way. The small-built, deceptively strong man lifted his end of the bed frame with its heavy oak headboard and carried it into the house with his partner. The house, with furniture coming and going, looked as if it had been hit by a hurricane.

Just like his life, Blaine thought.

It could have been a great deal worse. He looked toward his son sitting at the kitchen table. There couldn't have been a more sweet-tempered boy on the face of God's earth, Blaine thought. Mickey was methodically working his way around the peanut butter-and-jam sandwich his grandfather Jack—Blaine's father-in-law—had made for him. He was biting off the crust before getting down to the heart of it.

Blaine crossed his arms before his chest as he watched Mickey. He could feel his heart swelling. His son. His. Maybe this wouldn't be so bad after all.

Not that he had ever entertained negative thoughts about fatherhood. Just insecure ones. But Mickey was a good kid.

How hard could it be? he mused. After all, he'd been a boy himself once.

Blaine's mouth curved. According to his mother, sister and any neighbor within a five-mile radius of his old home, he'd been a hellion for the first fourteen years of his life. Even later, as he matured, he'd gotten away with a great deal because of his looks.

Not that he had been bad, either, Blaine thought, just…lively.

Blaine grinned to himself.

The bottom line was that he had been nothing at all like Mickey.

Who was he kidding? Blaine thought as he crossed to the counter and poured a cup of coffee. Smiling at Mickey, he seated himself at the table opposite his son. He didn't know the first thing about being a father. He didn't understand Mickey's needs or anything that was required in raising a sensitive little boy.

Those issues had been left in Diane's hands. By Diane's mandate. He'd bristled at the idea to begin with, but later he'd been relieved. The idea of disciplining, of ever having to say no to Mickey, made Blaine think of being the heavy. He was much better suited to the role of being the friend.

Diane had inadvertently done them a disservice, both him *and* Mickey. By taking complete control, she had left Blaine woefully unprepared for this unexpected turn of events.

She'd shut him out, Blaine knew, to get even with him. To pay him back for imagined wrongs that she was constantly conjuring up in a mind consumed with jealousy. Like the frightened child who saw ghosts in every darkened corner of her room, Diane saw indiscretions everywhere. She was positive of their existence, convicting Blaine because of his looks and his profession.

Diane had been pretty, like a wildflower growing in the meadow. But she had felt outclassed by the women who populated Blaine's world. As a magazine photographer, Blaine had immortalized some of the world's most beautiful women on the covers of popular magazines.

When they had first met, Diane had thought that his career was exciting, romantic and wondrously glamorous, even though he was only an apprentice at the time. By the time they divorced, she had considered it a sinful way of life that surrounded Blaine with temptation he was too weak to resist. She'd resented his work the way women resented their husband's mistresses.

He had tried to reassure her every time a bout of insecurity seized her. But her tantrums had only grown worse and worse and the air would grow thick with the accusations of infidelity she would hurl at him.

And then the ultimatum had come. He could either have her, or his career. He couldn't have both.

Blaine had never been one to be backed into a corner. Angry at her lack of trust, at the shallow view she had taken of his moral character, Blaine had chosen his career over his jealous wife.

He'd told himself he was better off without her, even though he still loved her. He couldn't continue to endure the daily fights, the vile recriminations. Or the scenes when they were out in public.

But despite all of that, when he discovered from his father-in-law that Diane was carrying his baby, Blaine was willing to give his marriage one last try. He'd even entertained the idea of finding another career if that was what it took to reassure her.

He could have saved his breath. Diane had taken great delight in telling him what he could do with his "last try."

He'd given her time, hoping she would change her mind. He had hoped all the way up to the moment the final divorce papers had arrived. It had been Jack who had called him from the hospital telling him he was the father of an eight-pound baby boy.

Blaine had been more than generous in the divorce settlement, making certain that his son would want for nothing. But his easygoing manner had changed when it came to visitation rights. Then he had hung on like a junkyard dog with the only bone in town, threatening to take Diane to court if necessary. She hadn't wanted him to have any rights at all.

Once again, it had been Jack who had won her over and gotten Diane to acquiesce. Jack had argued that a boy needed to see his father, to have his father in his life, however cursorily.

Blaine had always gotten along with Jack. He'd always managed to get along with almost everyone. Except, it seemed,

Diane. Diane, who saw nubile, scantily clad women in every closet, under every bed.

Diane, who had ruined what could have been a beautiful marriage. At least, beautiful was the way Blaine had once envisioned his marriage to be.

But now he knew better. He wasn't destined for marriage.

Maybe the breakup had been half his fault, he thought now with a posthumous wave of guilt. Maybe he had been too friendly with his models, too outgoing, too enthusiastic about his work. For whatever reason, Diane had misconstrued, misunderstood and misread until the tiny fissures in their marriage had become major faults that brought about an earthquake.

There was no use going over old ground again. There would be no mending of any fences with Diane now. A cross-country trucker who had fallen asleep at the wheel had seen to that.

Blaine hadn't been here for the news. Or the funeral. He'd come home three days ago from a shoot abroad and pressed the Play button on his answering machine, then gone numb at the knees as he listened. He had melted into a chair, staring in disbelief at the machine. He'd sat there a long time, staring.

Diane had been killed instantly.

All Blaine could think of, over and over again, was thank God Mickey hadn't been with her. It was only later, after his brain had thawed out and after he'd called Jack to offer his condolences, that he'd wondered: What was he going to do now?

He had known once, or, in his naiveté, had *thought* he'd known. Ten years ago, Blaine had been all set to be a father, even though he had felt a little shaky at the prospect.

But since then he'd had a great deal of time to become more set in his ways, more entrenched in a bachelor life that was, by definition, solitary. He came and went as he pleased and thought nothing of picking up and going off on a shoot for weeks at a time. There wasn't a plant in his apartment that needed watering, or a lonesome puppy to hand over to a helpful neighbor. There were no strings, no attachments in his life, save Mickey. And Diane had been responsible for him. Like the wind, Blaine could rustle in and out, leaving behind only a ripple.

But that was all changed now. The wind didn't have a ten-year-old son to take care of.

Blaine looked over his steaming cup of coffee at Mickey. They hadn't really talked very much since he had returned to Bedford. He'd held him and hugged him, but they hadn't really talked. Not even today. There was something forebodingly solemn about Mickey that had Blaine at a loss as to what to say.

Blaine had been here all morning, directing the moving men who were bringing in his possessions and removing some of the pieces that Diane had bought after the divorce. Diane had left everything to Mickey, including the house. Though he would have preferred to remain on his own terrain, Blaine was moving into his son's life rather than vice versa. He and Jack had discussed it and agreed that this way would be less unsettling than having Mickey move into his apartment, transferring schools and giving up friends at a time when he needed to be surrounded with the familiar.

What was going on in that little head? Blaine wondered. Mickey wasn't what could be termed an outgoing boy by nature, but Diane's death had made him so withdrawn, Blaine was concerned.

He studied the small, round face closely. "You okay?"

Mickey looked up at his father with rounded dark eyes that reminded Blaine of two shiny black marbles. His feet swung back and forth beneath the table like unsyncopated windshield wiper blades. One thin shoulder rose and fell as he continued to slowly chew his sandwich, as if he were thinking each bite through to its conclusion before taking the next.

"Yeah, I'm okay."

This wasn't easy for Blaine. Laughter had always been the hallmark of the times he and Mickey spent together. Deep-seated, darker emotions were part of a place Blaine had never ventured into with his son.

"Because if you're not okay—" Blaine stumbled over his tongue, searching for the right words like a jeweler searching for the perfect stone. Blaine tried again, "If you want to talk about it, we can."

There was just the tiniest hint of a cleft in the chin that Mickey raised, his eyes innocently puzzled. "It?" Mickey echoed quietly.

Blaine licked his lips, fervently wishing he was better at this. His talent was in framing photographs, not paragraphs.

He and Diane had gone from being lovers to being antagonists, but he had made certain that none of the animosity spilled over on Mickey. He'd never made derogatory statements about Diane when Mickey was with him. There had been no veiled vilifications or recriminations, no soft underhanded attempt to make Mickey choose sides. Mickey was too precious to taint with what had gone down between Diane and him. As far as Mickey knew, Blaine was as upset about his mother's death as he was.

"Your mom's—" Blaine searched for a euphemism, something he could use in place of that horrid five-letter word. But there was only one way to approach the issue. Honesty. "Death."

Mickey's black lashes swept his cheek as he looked down at his feet. He laid the remainder of his sandwich down on the plate. A small crescent was left.

"No," Mickey said quietly. "I'm okay."

The hell he was, Blaine thought. But all he could do was be here for him.

And love him, he thought.

Blaine reached across the table and squeezed his son's hand. Mickey looked up, a faint, sad smile on his lips. There was love in the boy's eyes, love granted without reservation, without qualifications.

God, he hoped he was up to this. He'd never had a responsibility before that even came close to equaling this.

"Hey, buddy," the shorter of the two moving men called to Blaine from the hall. His biceps bulged as they strained to keep up his end of the bureau. As he stopped, he tilted it so that it was leaning into him. The burly man nodded at the piece of furniture, which appeared to be cradled against him like a sleeping child on his mother's bosom. "You want this in the same place as the other piece?"

Blaine nodded vaguely. "Yes, put it in the master bedroom." His mind wasn't on his furniture. It was on his son.

They'd made this arrangement, he and Jack, because they both thought it best for Mickey. Jack, a retired police officer, was going to remain with them for at least a month to help out. But Jack had been more than willing to take the boy to his house if a transition period was needed. Mickey, when consulted, had opted to remain here. Little boys were known to change their minds, though.

Blaine leaned toward Mickey, creating an air of confidentiality. "Are you sure you didn't want to stay with Grandpa for a while?"

Mickey wrapped his hands around the glass of milk before him, but he made no move to drink.

"You." His voice was barely above a whisper. "I want to stay with you." He swallowed before raising his eyes to his father's face. Hope and fear chose their battleground there. "Unless you don't want me."

Blaine's mug met the table surface with a thud as he rose from the chair. He circumvented the table to Mickey's side. Leaning against the table, he placed his hands on the small shoulders.

"Don't you ever, ever think that."

His tone was far harsher than he believed himself capable of with Mickey. Harsh and choked with emotion. What sort of trash had Diane filled his son's head with? he wondered angrily. Had she told the little boy his father didn't care in order to make him choose sides? He might have refrained from making references about Diane in the boy's presence, but Blaine knew that the arrangement had not been reciprocated by the small things the boy would occasionally let drop.

"I want you." His eyes held his son's. "I have always wanted you. I *will* always want you." His voice softened. "Understand?"

Mickey blinked, then, slowly, the solemn expression on his face faded in intensity as he nodded. "Yes, I understand."

Blaine released his son's shoulders, aware that he might have been holding him a little too tightly.

"It's not going to be easy," Blaine said after a moment.

Easy? God, it was going to be downright hard, he thought, but he could manage it. He'd already taken the first major step. He'd moved back into the house. A house full of memories, not only for Mickey, but for him. It was here where he and Diane had begun their marriage. And here where it had died that awful, rainy Thursday night, when he had walked out for the last time.

She'd kept the house after the divorce for the same reason she had kept him away from Mickey as much as possible. To spite him because he had cared about it.

"But we're going to manage," Blaine promised Mickey now, with a great deal more certainty than he felt. "He—ck." At the last moment, he switched the word that had naturally sprung to his lips. He was going to have to curb his language now, he thought. Another change. But Mickey was worth it. The boy was worth everything. "With Grandpa here to help out," Blaine continued, "we'll be just like the family on 'My Three Sons.'" He laughed and amended, "Minus a couple of sons, of course."

"Huh?" Mickey's expression told Blaine that he had lost his way.

It took Blaine a moment to remember that Diane hadn't allowed the boy to watch television. She'd called it a waste of time. Mickey had never had the opportunity to catch the classic sixties program in reruns.

"Never mind, that'll be part of your education," he promised. Between classic cartoons in syndication and selected other programs Blaine had already mentally earmarked for Mickey, the boy had a lot of catching up to do.

He cupped the boy's cheek, the wonder of his new situation not fully registering, yet. He had a son depending on him now. Full time. It still took his breath away when he thought about it.

Blaine dropped his hand and straightened. As he took Mickey's dish and his own drained coffee mug to the sink, he heard an unsettling *thud* coming from the general direction of the master bedroom. He winced and wondered if wood glue could rectify whatever had just happened.

He looked down at Mickey, who was shadowing his every step. "So, you're sure you don't want to talk about, uh, anything?"

"Sure," Mickey echoed. He underlined his statement with a nod of his head.

Blaine wasn't convinced. Mickey couldn't be as calm as he appeared. Could he?

Having rinsed the plate without looking, Blaine placed it on the rack. "Well, I'm here for you if you do decide that you want to talk or—something."

Blaine shoved his hands into his pockets as he went out to see how the movers were faring. God, he was going to make a mess of it, he thought with a wave of anxiety. He just knew it.

But Blaine knew that all he could do was place one foot in front of the other and pray that he didn't step on anything.

She hated funerals, absolutely hated them.

Bridgette Rafanelli knew that it had been cowardly of her. But she hadn't been able to make herself attend the funeral, even though Diane had been a friend.

No, Bridgette amended fiercely, *because* Diane had been a friend. There was something altogether spirit-shredding about listening to final words being said about a person who had been alive and vibrant only a few days ago.

She couldn't go.

Funerals reminded her of when she had lost her mother. Then she had been forced to stand between her father and Nonna, listening to a white-haired priest saying words about someone she would never see again. Nonna had held on to her hand tightly, silently offering her a wealth of comfort. It hadn't been enough. Bridgette remembered the church growing smaller and then disappearing. She had woken up on a cold, cracked leather sofa in the rectory, with her grandmother hovering over her.

Bridgette let out a long breath as she guided her car into a residential development. She might be short on courage when it came to standing and listening to eulogies, but she was long on compassion and love. Right now, Mickey O'Connor needed both.

There was a very special place in her heart for Mickey. With his dark, heart-melting looks and soulful black eyes, he looked exactly like photographs she'd seen of her uncle Gino when he was that age. Gino had only been two years older than Mickey when her father had left her with Nonna and him. That had been a year after Mama had died. Gino had been more like a big brother to her than an uncle. He'd brought a great deal of comfort and laughter into her life, as had Nonna.

It was time to pass on the favor.

She brought her white convertible to a stop at the curb. The driveway was blocked by a huge moving van. As she watched, two men in beige coveralls came out of the house, struggling with Diane's four-poster bed.

Was Mickey moving away?

Her mouth hardened as she remembered things Diane had told her about her ex-husband. The rat probably couldn't wait to sell her things and rent out the house. She thought of Mickey. He was so painfully shy. How was he going to adjust to so many changes?

By the time she approached the opened door and knocked on the jamb, Bridgette had accused, tried and convicted Blaine O'Connor of emotional child abuse.

Bridgette knocked again, fully expecting to look into Jack Robertson's weathered face. Nonna had attended the funeral to lend her emotional support to Jack. She'd been seeing Jack socially for almost a year now, thanks to Bridgette's introduction. Her grandmother had told her that Diane's father was going to be staying with Mickey until some sort of final arrangements could be made.

Obviously they'd been made faster than either one of them had anticipated.

Nonna hadn't mentioned that anyone else would be staying with Mickey. She certainly hadn't mentioned a tall, broad-shouldered man in a faded blue shirt and even more faded blue jeans. He had silky dark hair and troubled green eyes as he looked down at her.

She knew who he was immediately.

He looked like Mickey, except for the eyes. And except for the fact that innocence that was so blatantly stamped on Mickey's face had been chiseled out of Blaine's.

Bridgette attempted to swallow the animosity that instantly sprang up to seize her by the throat as fragments of things Diane had told her swam through her mind. She succeeded only marginally.

If she was selling something, Blaine thought, this raven-haired woman was going about it all wrong. The scowl on her face would have a lesser man quaking in his shoes, even if he was innocent.

But Blaine was well versed in accusing looks. Diane had been a master at them.

"Yes?"

Bridgette squared her shoulders as she unconsciously ran a hand through her hair. It was a nervous habit Nonna chided her for.

"I'm here to see Mickey."

The movers were approaching the house with Blaine's fifty-inch television set. Instinctively, he grasped the unknown woman by the shoulders and maneuvered her out of the way. He managed to draw her momentarily into the house.

As she pulled back, he looked at her curiously, humor curving his mouth. "I know he's a serious boy, but aren't you a little old for him?"

Bridgette didn't care for his cocky attitude, or the way he had handled her as if she were a chair, in the way. "Is there an age requirement for friends?"

He should have worn his parka for that one, he thought, a little amused at her retort. Pure frost. Who *was* she?

"No, of course not."

With a photographer's eye, he studied her for a moment. Blaine could envision her in a half dozen layouts. If the woman didn't model, she should. The nice thing about photographs, he mused, was that you never heard the model's voice. This one's was low and throaty. And accusing as hell.

"Now that you're in my house, would you mind if I asked who you are?"

His house? The man worked fast. "I'm Bridgette Rafanelli, Mickey's music teacher."

Another thing he wasn't aware of, he thought. He wondered how long Mickey had been taking lessons. He had just assumed that the piano in the living room was for show. Diane had always enjoyed putting on airs.

There were so many things about Mickey that he didn't know, he realized, frustration gnawing away at him.

Blaine extended his hand. "I'm Mickey's father, Blaine O'Connor."

Bridgette had every intention of ignoring his hand, but that would have made her as boorish as she knew he was. So instead, she thrust her hand into his and shook it tersely, then pulled it away, as if it were odious to touch him.

"I know."

By her judgmental tone, Blaine surmised that she had heard about him from Diane and that whatever she had heard was decidedly unflattering.

"That makes you one up on me." He slid his hands into his pockets as he kept one eye on the movers. He had no intention of allowing them to manhandle his set.

Blaine saw the frown on her mouth deepen. "I take it you were also a friend of Diane's."

"Yes."

Whatever Diane had said must have been horrid. Her voice fairly dripped with acrimony. Blaine felt annoyance rising at being prejudged this way. He opened his mouth to ask her what her problem was when she strode past him, her eyes on the piano.

She pointed toward it. "Are you leaving the piano?"

He came up behind her. He was almost a foot taller, he thought. "Yes."

"Good." She looked around. The house appeared in a state of utter chaos. And Mickey was nowhere to be seen. She turned around to look at Blaine and nearly bumped into him. Space was at a premium and somehow, he seemed to take up all of it. "May I see Mickey?"

Attitude. The lady exuded attitude. The wrong kind of attitude and he'd had just about enough of it. Blaine folded his arms before him as he studied her. He took his time answering, enjoying the fact that his drawl apparently seemed to annoy her.

"You can if you tell me why you sound as if your tongue is a sword and I'm the pumice stone you're determined to sharpen it on."

Diane had said he was charming and Bridgette could see it, in a rough sort of way. That only intensified her adverse reaction to him. "Diane told me a great deal about you."

Blaine's easy gaze narrowed. "And you've decided that only pure gospel passed Diane's lips."

"I don't see much to contradict her." She gestured toward

the movers. They were taking out Diane's white marble-topped table. "You're getting rid of her things."

He didn't see how this was any business of hers. "Just some of them. So that I can move mine in."

She looked at him in surprise. "You're moving in?"

He liked the way surprise rounded her mouth. It was an interesting mouth, he decided. Under other circumstances, perhaps even a tempting mouth. "To be with my son." He emphasized each word.

For a moment, Blaine's statement took some of the indignant wind out of her sails. Diane had maintained that Blaine wanted to have no part of his son. This was a twist she hadn't expected.

"Blaine, I thought I'd take Mickey and run to the store." A gravely voice boomed out, announcing Jack Robertson's appearance. "You mind watching this four-legged nuisance while we're gone?"

The dog in question, a three-year-old German shepherd named Spangles that had been a gift from Blaine, barked in protest, as if knowing he was under discussion.

Jack halted abruptly when he saw that his former son-in-law had company. Didn't take the man long, Jack thought without resentment. What Blaine and Diane had had died a long time ago. He couldn't be faulted for getting on with his life.

And then the woman turned around and Jack grinned broadly, his tanned face dissolving into creases and lines that Nonna had confided to Bridgette were "sexy."

He put his hands out and took both of Bridgette's in his. "Hello, Bridgette. We missed you at the funeral."

Uncomfortable, Bridgette lifted a shoulder and then let it fall. She resisted the temptation of dragging a hand through her hair. She supposed that there was no excuse for not attending the funeral. She had even gone so far as to get dressed in a somber navy blue dress and gotten in behind the wheel of her car.

But at the end, she couldn't bring herself to drive to the

church. She couldn't even turn on the ignition. If she wasn't there for the service, for the interment, then some part of her could go on believing that Diane was still alive.

"Diane knew how I felt about funerals. She would have understood." Bridgette placed her arms around the older man. "Jack, I'm so very sorry."

He patted her shoulder, determined not to break down. It wasn't the way he saw himself. Tears were for private moments when he was alone.

"Me, too, Bridgette. Me, too."

The sad moment was dissolved as a high voice squealed. "Bridgette, you're here."

Bridgette just had time to step away from Jack before she found her waist engulfed as Mickey threw his arms around her.

She laughed as she hugged him to her. "I sure am, sweetheart."

Blaine could only look on in awe. It was the most emotional display he'd seen from Mickey since the accident.

His eyes met Bridgette's over Mickey's head. There was just a trace of a smug smile on her lips.

Chapter Two

Bridgette held Mickey against her. She ached for him when she thought of what his young heart had to endure. Death was always difficult to cope with, but it seemed so much more brutal when it invaded the life of a child. More than anything, she wished that there was something she could do for him.

Without thinking, she stroked his hair, just the way she'd seen Diane do a hundred times before.

Mickey pulled away from her with a jerk, as if something had suddenly snapped shut within him. The impression wasn't negated when Bridgette looked down at him. The friendliness was gone, wiped away like a chalk drawing on the sidewalk in the rain. In its place there was a somber cast in his eyes which brought a chill to her heart.

"Mickey?"

Hand extended, Bridgette took a step toward him, then stopped. She had the definite feeling that she was intruding.

Never forgetting what her own childhood was like, both the good and the bad, Bridgette prided herself on being instinctively good with children. It was a gift rather than something she had to nurture. She truly enjoyed their company and they sensed it and responded to her. Especially shy children like Mickey.

This reaction was something she was entirely unprepared for.

Mickey licked his lips and shrugged, his shoulders moving independently of each other. He looked uneasy, lost. Looking down at the floor, he shoved his hands deep into his pockets.

"I got my video game on pause," he mumbled to the rug. "I can't keep it that way or it'll get ruined. That's what Mom says. Said. I gotta go."

Mickey turned and fled. Spangles followed like a four-legged shadow.

Bridgette could have sworn she'd heard Mickey's voice crack, though his expression had remained frozen, unemotional. It was all the motivation she needed. But as she began to follow after him, a hand fell on her shoulder, preventing her.

Just barely suppressing her annoyance, she looked up at Blaine.

He waited a moment before he dropped his hand from her shoulder. "Maybe he just needs to work this out for himself."

That would be the path he'd take, she thought. Noninterference. Translation: Do nothing, just as he had been doing all along. The man hadn't a clue as to what Mickey needed.

"He's ten years old. He doesn't *know* how to work this out for himself," she shot back. "What he needs is to be held."

With the bearing of a man who knew an altercation in the making when he saw one, Jack physically placed himself between them. "What he needs is not to hear two adults arguing over him."

Bridgette flushed as she turned toward Jack, embarrassed at having taken the safety latch off her temper. But she was a passionate woman who took each emotion she was experiencing to the limit.

Ignoring Blaine, she placed her hand on Jack's arm. Comfort seemed to flow from her very fingertips. "I'm sorry, Jack. I guess my emotions just got the better of me." She knew Jack understood. She wasn't all that different from her grandmother. "Is there anything I can do for you or Mickey?"

Jack shook his head, a bittersweet smile on his lips. Bridgette meant well, but there wasn't anything she could do. Nothing anyone could do, really.

"You can give us time, honey." He patted the hand on his arm, knowing that she was in need of comfort herself. She'd lost a friend she'd cared about. "That's the only thing that's going to help. Time. Putting one foot in front of the other and getting from here to there."

He was right. She knew that from experience. Still, she wished there was something she could do. Something that didn't make her feel so useless, so frustrated. Especially when it involved Mickey.

Bridgette blew out a breath. "Well, if you think of anything, I'm here." She looked in the direction that Mickey had gone.

She really didn't have to say it, but it was nice to hear. "I know." Jack fought back the clawing emotion that threatened to overwhelm him. Tears, he knew, were going to be a part of his life for a long time to come. But he refused to give in to them except in his room at night. So he forced a smile to his lips for everyone's sake, including his own. "Tell Sophia I appreciated the casseroles. I didn't really feel like cooking."

If anyone could help him through this, Bridgette knew her grandmother could. Zestful and vivacious even though she was well through her fifth decade, Sophia Rafanelli had the enthusiasm for life of a woman one-third her age. Nonna had seen Bridgette through the darkest parts of her life.

"You can tell her yourself. She plans to come by this evening."

Jack nodded, visibly brightening. "Great." Emotion threatened to take hold of him. He thought he'd be better off alone just now. Jack edged his way to the hall. "I'll see you later."

Nonna would help Jack, Bridgette mused as the man left the room. But who or what was going to help Mickey?

The answer was plain. She was.

Bridgette took a step toward the hall, only to feel the same hand on her shoulder, laying a bit more heavily this time. Annoyance leapt up again. She glared at his hand as if it were a disembodied limb until he removed it.

The woman had a look that could ignite wet kindling, Blaine thought as he dropped his hand to his side. "I'd rather that you didn't go there right now."

There was no point in playing innocent. They both knew she meant to go to Mickey's room. "Why?"

Blaine saw no reason to give her any explanations. "He's my son," he answered flatly.

It amazed Bridgette that he didn't stumble over the word. It was certainly foreign enough to him. Everything that Diane had told her about him rose up at once, crowding her mind.

"That's not a reason, that's a fact." Her eyes narrowed as she looked up at him. "One that didn't seem to trouble you before."

Blaine had no idea what this woman was talking about, nor why he even cared. But puzzles had always drawn him in. "Excuse me?"

Didn't he care how all this affected Mickey? Hadn't it occurred to him that Mickey had needed him before this day? "I don't remember seeing you coming around."

The woman's gall took his breath away. She certainly outdistanced Diane when it came to nerve. "I didn't know I was supposed to check in with you."

Bridgette saw temper flaring in his eyes. Hers rose higher. It was fueled by her feelings for Mickey and by the indignities that Diane had confided she'd suffered. Bridgette was surprised that Blaine even had the nerve to show his face after all this time. Most of all, she was surprised that Jack wasn't making plans to ride him out on a rail. But then, Jack had always been a very kind man.

"From what I gathered, it wouldn't have been often." Bridgette turned on her heel. She made it all the way across the threshold before Blaine grabbed her arm and turned her around to face him.

"Just a minute. I think I'd like a word with you." The defiant look on her face made him think of a winter storm about to break. If she thought he was going to back off because of it, she was in for a surprise. "A very long word."

"All right." Bridgette pulled her arm away and then folded both in front of her. "I'm listening." Not that anything he had to say would make a difference in the way she felt, she added silently.

She was pushing buttons that brought back scenes from his marriage. But Blaine held his ground instead of ignoring her and walking away. This wasn't Diane. This was some crazy woman who thought she had a place in his son's life. Why, he didn't know.

"I don't even really know who the hell you are, lady."

Bridgette gave a short laugh. "I'm surprised Mickey didn't say the same thing to you when you showed up, omitting the 'lady' part, of course."

The word *shrew* leapt to his mind. But that wasn't unexpected, seeing as how she and Diane had been friends.

"My son knows who I am."

"Long-term memory, no doubt."

Blaine curbed the very real desire to take her by the arms and shake her until she made some sense. "Did you come here to go a few rounds with me for some warped reason?"

The moving men were looking at them. They'd stopped working and were obviously very entertained by what was transpiring. Taking her by the arm, he ushered her none-too-gently back into the living room as he mentally cursed himself for losing his temper like this. He was an easygoing man who hardly ever raised his voice. Diane had been the only one who had ever made him shout.

Until now.

Hanging on to what was left of her temper, Bridgette waved a dismissive hand at Blaine.

"I didn't even know you were here. I just came by to see how Jack and Mickey were doing." She paused for a moment as she looked him squarely in the eye. "Mickey obviously isn't doing very well."

Exasperation shouted for release. Just who did she think she was, coming here and passing judgment? "His mother just died, what do you expect him to be? Practicing cartwheels for a circus act?" A loud noise in the background reminded him of the movers, as well as of Jack and Mickey. With effort, he lowered his voice again. "All things considered, he's doing rather well."

"Oh, really?"

She tossed her hair over her shoulder. The slight action looked like a challenge from where he stood. Her hands balled into fists at her waist didn't do anything to dispel that impression.

"And just what is your definition of 'well'?" The man was not only heartless, he was blind to boot, Bridgette thought.

For two cents, he'd gladly clip that raised chin of hers. "Not that it's any business of yours, Ms. Fanelli—"

"*Raf*anelli," she corrected tersely.

"Ms. *Raf*anelli," he echoed in the same tone she'd used, "My definition of *well* is the way Mickey is handling it. He's behaving calmly, like an adult."

There were words for dunderheads like O'Connor, but she refrained from using them. She didn't want Mickey hearing her swear. But she had to bite her lip, physically holding back the barrage. When she finally spoke, it was in a low, barely controlled voice.

"You probably missed this piece of information in your vast travels around the globe, but Mickey is only ten. He's not supposed to act like an adult until he's past puberty." Her eyes washed over Blaine. The look in them was far from flattering, even though she wasn't oblivious to the fact that he was a very good-looking man. "Of course, for some it's a reversed process."

He'd had enough of her sarcasm. "Look, I really don't have time for this—"

That had been the excuse Diane said he always used when she called him, asking him to come see his son. "Don't have time for very much except your work, do you?"

The image of wrapping his hands around her throat seemed to spring up out of nowhere. He wasn't a violent man by nature. Nonetheless, it was a very pleasing image.

"Not that I really care about your opinion, but just what is that supposed to mean?" Before Bridgette could respond, he added, "For that matter, what are all of your sarcastic remarks supposed to mean?" It took a great deal to keep from lashing out at her. "You don't even *know* me."

That's where he was wrong. Bridgette set her mouth hard. Diane had told her plenty about this man, the heartache he'd caused her, the pain. "I know enough."

There was a steely look in his eyes. His tone dropped. It was harsh, devoid of emotion, as if it had all been spent. Or kept under lock and key. "From Diane."

Blaine saw her raise her head, as if to defend the dead woman. Diane might be gone, but it seemed that her staff had been taken up by another. Even dead she knew how to make his life difficult. "Well, did it ever occur to you that perhaps she colored things a little? Or a lot, as the case may be."

She wouldn't have expected him to say anything else. But Bridgette had facts at her disposal. "You were in London for Christmas."

The statement was worded like an accusation. "What does—?"

She didn't let him finish. "And you were in the Philippines, doing layouts for the ever famous swimsuit issue for Mickey's tenth birthday."

That had been unavoidable. He'd been facing an ironclad deadline. But he had managed to call Mickey and talk to him at length. Only because Jack had answered the telephone. Had it been Diane, he would have never had the opportunity to talk to the boy. He and Mickey had celebrated the day a week later. Royally.

"Yes, but—"

She ignored his attempt at a protest. Nothing he could say would negate the facts. "On Mickey's first birthday, you were—" She looked up at him innocently. "Where was it again?"

Blaine shoved his hands into his pockets much the way Mickey had. "Canada. Quebec." He grounded out the answer through clenched teeth. He remembered being very lonely that day. He'd missed Mickey something fierce. "Is this a trial?"

It was a rhetorical question. She had obviously already convicted him and was leading him to the gallows.

She wished Jack hadn't left. She felt better talking to him, not arguing with this biological miscreant. "No, I'm merely substantiating my point."

Blaine's expression hardened, hiding the anger boiling just beneath. "Which is?"

"That what Diane told me was true."

Leave it to Diane to skip the part about how he made it up to Mickey. How he always found a way to make it up to Mickey. The nature of his work didn't allow him the freedom to live like most men. That was both the beauty and the burden of his career. And even if he hadn't had that career, there'd always been Diane to act as a stumbling block.

"Yes, but—"

Her eyes dared him to deny what she was saying. "There is no 'but' here, O'Connor. It's either true or it's not and you just said it was, thereby dismissing your earlier insinuation that Diane lied about you."

Why he was even bothering to stand here, arguing with her,

within earshot of his father-in-law and the movers, was beyond him. Maybe it was the fact that he had never managed to convince Diane that he was innocent that goaded him on to make her understand.

"Look, before you pass judgment on me—"

He had told her what she wanted to know and she didn't care to stand around, listening to him attempt to talk his way out of it.

Her eyes were cold as they appraised him. She could see why Diane had fallen for him. He was tall, muscular and had a definite sexual air about him that would have been appealing if she didn't know what she did about him.

"I'm not passing judgment. I couldn't care less what you do or where you go. I do, however, care a great deal about Mickey."

"Why?" She wasn't a relative. He saw no reason for her to be so adamant about the boy.

She debated ignoring his question, then relented. "For a lot of reasons. For one, I'm his godmother."

It took him a moment to assimilate her words. Diane had deliberately planned Mickey's christening to take place while he was away. As always, he hadn't found out about the ceremony until after the fact.

"You are?"

His ignorance of the fact didn't surprise her. Diane had said he had cut himself off from his son's life except for the mandatory child support payments. And even they were late in coming.

"Didn't know that, either, did you?"

The tally against this man was adding up. He was an absentee father, just like her own had been. Oh, Carlo Rafanelli had been there physically, providing a roof over her head and food for her sustenance. But emotionally, where it counted, it was as if he didn't exist. Or she didn't. And when he had remarried, he had moved away, leaving her in Nonna's care. In the end, he'd gone on with his life as if he'd never had a daughter at all.

Standing here, talking to this thickheaded, thick-skinned oaf, brought it all back to her.

Well, maybe she thought she had some right to interfere in Mickey's welfare, but not in Blaine's book. Especially not with that attitude. "As his godmother, it would have been your obligation to look after Mickey if both his parents were gone."

It was on the tip of her tongue to say that they might as well have been for all the difference he made, but she bit it back.

There, he thought with a small measure of triumph, that seemed to have managed to shut her up. "As it happens, I'm very much alive and intend to take care of Mickey on my own."

She had no idea why he was here—possibly to ease his conscience, or maybe just to sell off Diane's furniture. But there was no doubt in her mind that the man Diane had told her about would soon be off somewhere. Without Mickey in tow. Seeing as how he was a philandering womanizer, that would probably be all to the good.

Bridgette nodded, making no attempt to hide her skepticism. "Fine. How?"

There seemed to be no end to this woman's audacity. "Excuse me?"

"How?" she repeated, slowly mouthing the word as if she were talking to someone with greatly diminished mental capacities. "What are your plans for him?"

He had barely gotten his head together and accepted the facts that Diane was dead and that he was a full-time father and had to change his entire life around. Restructuring Mickey's life was something he hadn't gotten around to, yet.

Blaine waved his hand around in frustration. "Beyond sending him to school tomorrow, I haven't thought that out, yet."

She was forced to step out of the way and toward him as the movers brought in a rather scarred-looking credenza. As soon as she could, she moved aside. She didn't like standing so close to him. There was too much charged tension in the air.

"So, you plan to live here with him?"

"Yes." He nodded, then shrugged. That, too, was up in the air. "For now."

He made it sound tentative. Mickey needed stability. He needed a lot of things, especially a loving father, but at the very least, he needed stability. O'Connor owed him that much. If he didn't think so, he was badly mistaken. And Bridgette would be the one to show him.

"I think you should try to make life as normal as possible for him."

That was exactly why he was moving in. So why was hearing it from her lips setting his teeth on edge? Right about now, if she said snow was white, he would be tempted to shout that it was black.

"What you think is completely irrelevant to me, Ms.—look, what's your first name again?"

"Bridgette." She didn't want him calling her by her first name. She wanted their relationship to remain completely formal. "Ms. Rafanelli will do just fine."

The absence of Ms. Rafanelli would do even better, he thought. It was time to get on with the rest of his life and get her out of here. He took her elbow. "Well, thanks for coming."

Bridgette eluded his hold. "I'd like to say goodbye to Mickey."

If he let her go, there was no telling when she would leave. "I'll tell him for you."

The hell he would, she thought.

"Thanks, but I'd rather do it myself."

With that, she hurried down the hall before he attempted to forcibly eject her. She wouldn't put it past him. Any man who could neglect a child was capable of almost anything.

Bridgette stopped just short of Mickey's doorway. Singsong music was coming out of the room. The door was slightly ajar. She pushed it open slowly with her fingertips. Inside, Mickey was sitting on the floor in front of a small portable television set. He was as erect as if a ruler had been inserted under his hockey team T-shirt. Bridgette quietly slipped into the room.

Mickey didn't even notice her presence. His eyes were focused on the colorful screen, his finger mechanically pumping the buttons on the control pad.

He didn't seem to be in the room at all.

Cry, Mickey, cry.

On-screen, a tiny gnome in green livery was valiantly attempting to rescue an equally tiny princess in a far-off castle. The gnome kept falling into the moat. Each time he did, another one of his lives was lost.

"How many points do you have?" she asked softly.

Mickey didn't bother to turn around. It was as if he'd known she was there all the time. Known and hadn't reacted. "Nine hundred and three. But I've only got one life left."

He usually played very well. And likely as not, he would ask her to join him. He made no such request today.

"Better be careful then."

There was nothing left to say for the moment. Mickey had completely withdrawn into himself. Maybe Jack was right. Maybe Mickey did need a little time to himself first. "I'm going home now."

Mickey nodded. The gnome fell into the moat again. The sign Game Over flashed. He started a new game.

She wanted to sweep him into her arms again. To hold him and rock him and let him cry his heart out. Stymied, she remained where she was.

"If you need anything, my telephone number is number three on the ReDial." She'd helped Diane program it. Diane had always been so lost when it came to anything remotely complicated. "Call me anytime if you need to talk."

Mickey nodded again. She knew he wouldn't be calling. At least, not for a while.

Bridgette felt awkward. She had never felt awkward with a

child before, but then, there was the aura of a third party in the room with them. Death made her feel uncomfortable and at a loss.

"Anyway," she said, backing up toward the door, "I'll see you tomorrow after school for lessons."

"Okay," he mumbled to his control pad.

Bridgette was desperate to get any sort of reaction from Mickey. It was as if that one moment when he'd first seen her had been a slip. She saw no trace of the boy she knew. "We can go over a new song."

"Okay."

She sighed inwardly and retreated. She'd try again tomorrow. "'Bye."

He glanced at her for a moment, a troubled, lost soul, before returning to his game. "'Bye."

Feeling frustrated beyond words, Bridgette turned and walked directly into Blaine. He'd been standing right outside Mickey's room, obviously listening to every word. Needing a target, she selected him.

Bridgette pushed Blaine away, trying not to notice that she had experienced a definite reaction to brushing up against his very hard body.

"Why are you hovering over me?" she whispered angrily as she stepped to the side so that Mickey couldn't hear them.

He had a question of his own. "Why are you coming back tomorrow?"

She had a feeling that he'd like nothing better than to bar her from Mickey's life. Fat chance.

"I already told you. Besides being his godmother, I'm also his piano teacher. We have a lesson tomorrow." She was determined to give the boy some semblance of order within the chaos he found himself in. It was a given that this man wouldn't.

"I'm canceling it. You don't have to come by." The last thing he needed while he was trying to establish a fuller relationship with Mickey was to have her around, sniping at him.

Oh, no, it wasn't going to be that easy. It wasn't going to be easy at all. Getting rid of her was going to be downright impossible, she promised him silently. She had an emotional stake in Mickey. For his sake and Diane's, she intended to be around.

"I'm paid up through the end of the month," she informed him as she crossed to the front door. "I'll be back." She paused in the doorway and looked at him over her shoulder. "Some of us still honor commitments."

There was no denying the fact that the woman was gorgeous, just as there was no denying the fact that she was a shrew. A pity.

"And some of you need to be committed," he muttered under his breath.

She grinned for the first time since she had entered. "Exactly. 'Bye, Jack," she called out. "I'm leaving."

Not far away enough, Blaine thought as he closed the door firmly behind her.

Jack walked in, too late to say goodbye. He gathered by Blaine's expression that the meeting with Bridgette had gone from bad to worse after he'd left the room. The fact amused him. "She's something else, isn't she?"

Blaine turned, then made an effort to regain his composure. "That's putting it rather mildly."

Jack laughed as he led the way into the kitchen. "You should see her grandmother."

Blaine caught the fond note in Jack's voice. Jack had been a widower for as long as he'd known him. He had never thought of the man as being interested in finding a romantic partner. He wondered if Jack was being taken advantage of.

"Anything like her?"

Jack took out two mugs from the cupboard and set them on the counter. The expression on his face belonged to that of a man years younger. "Yes. A warm, passionate woman who makes you glad you're alive."

Blaine shook his head as he watched Jack pour coffee into his mug. "Then she's nothing at all like her granddaughter."

Jack lowered himself into the kitchen chair, then took a tentative sip of his coffee. He studied his former son-in-law over the rim of his mug. "Bridgette was very close to Diane."

Blaine had already gathered that. He joined Jack at the table. "She looks like she wants to get close to me, too." He saw the quizzical look in Jack's eyes. "With a hatchet."

Though he loved his daughter, Jack had been very aware that Diane had had her shortcomings. "Diane might have told her a few things—"

Now *there* was an understatement. "If she had told Bridgette that I was the Boston Strangler and Bluebeard rolled up into one, I still would have had a warmer reception."

Blaine didn't know Bridgette the way he did. "Bridgette's just worried about Mickey."

"Well, so am I," Blaine snapped. He realized that he was letting his own tension spill out. Maybe that was why he'd balked at what Bridgette said, as well. No, he amended, the woman had merited his reaction. But Jack didn't.

He sighed, leaning back in his chair. "Jack, I have no idea how to be a father."

Jack laughed softly under his breath. "When you find out, you can let the rest of us in on it." Mentally, he postponed his trip to the store. It was time to walk Spangles. Mickey would probably enjoy that more. He rose stiffly and clamped a hand on Blaine's shoulder. "Mostly it's just flying by the seat of your pants and hoping you don't crash-land."

Blaine shook his head. That wasn't the way he saw it. "My dad always seemed to know what to do, what to say. He was never at a loss in any situation."

Then he'd be the first, Jack thought. "Your dad was just good at playacting. Fathers only pretend to know what they're talking about." He considered Blaine the son he'd never had.

"Remember, every father was once a little boy. It'll work out, Blaine. It's just going to take time. If it makes you feel any better, I'll hang around for as long as it takes for you to get comfortable with this."

Blaine knew it was the coward's way out, but right now, he wasn't feeling all that brave about the situation. And talking to Bridgette had just made it worse. "Thanks, I appreciate that."

Jack easily dismissed his thanks. "And don't be too hard on Bridgette. She loves Mickey a lot."

Why did he get this feeling that it was a competition between them? "So do I."

Jack winked, amused at Blaine's tone. "That gives you something in common."

Blaine set his empty mug down and pretended to shiver. "Now that's a scary thought."

Jack laughed again. It was good to begin to feel alive again. He had three other daughters, but Diane had been his baby. Perhaps he had always favored her because, of all his children, she'd been the one who needed it most, the one with so many insecurities. For whatever the reason, he'd closed his eyes to a lot of her faults.

"After I walk Spangles, I'll help you hook up your VCR."

Blaine looked at him in surprise. "You know how to do that?"

Jack pretended to take umbrage at Blaine's tone. "Hell, not everyone over fifty is a dinosaur." He squinted a little as he focused on Blaine. "I could probably beat you at that video game as well."

"Probably." Blaine's smile faded a little. "Jack?"

Jack took a box of dog biscuits out of the cupboard and pocketed one. Sometimes, Spangles had to be coaxed to head for home. "Yeah?"

Blaine knew he was lucky to have help at a time like this. "Thanks for being here."

Gratitude always made him uncomfortable, as if he were wearing a scratchy sweater.

"My pleasure, Blaine, my pleasure." And then he smiled. "I always did like you."

Blaine nodded. "Too bad Diane didn't."

Jack nodded as he left the kitchen. "Yeah, too bad."

Chapter Three

It seemed rather unusual to Blaine, with all the things he had on his mind, that he would actually find himself thinking of Bridgette. Yet there she was, thrusting herself into his thoughts like a commuter pushing her way through a crowded subway car to reach the door.

And not just once—he could have dealt with it if it had been just once. No, she popped up, unannounced, unwanted, unbidden, several times within the small space of half a day. Considering that they didn't exactly hit it off on their first meeting, he couldn't understand why this was happening.

It was enough to make a sane man crazy.

Blaine glanced at Mickey sitting beside him on the sofa. Dinner had long since been over and Jack had gone out with Bridgette's grandmother, an attractive, vivacious woman who didn't deserve the term grandmother or, in Blaine's opinion, the ignoble honor of being related to Bridgette. That left the two of them alone in the house, if he didn't count the dog. He knew that it was important to establish a solid routine for Mickey. But Blaine's life had been anything but routine. It wasn't easy for him, not only adjusting to but laying down a schedule of some sort.

Desperately casting about for a starting point, Blaine had gladly abandoned his unpacking and coaxed Mickey into watching a television program with him. It was a short, snappy sitcom aimed at the family.

Twenty minutes into the program, that show had cut to a commercial for skin cream. The woman caressing the pink jar had an exquisite complexion that would have rivaled Snow White's.

The enticing pink hue that had crept up Bridgette's cheek earlier that day flashed through Blaine's mind like a bolt of lightning in a sudden summer thunderstorm.

He wondered what Diane had actually told her about him to bring about such an intense reaction from her. Whatever it was, it had to be a lie. He was going to have to set her straight.

Blaine sighed, annoyed with himself. Why did he even care what she thought? And why in heaven's name was she preying on his mind with the tenacity of a carnivorous jackal?

The answer, he supposed, was simple enough if he thought about it. She was returning tomorrow and he didn't want her to. The last thing he needed right now was recriminations or someone telling him what he was doing wrong. What he needed was someone to tell him what to do *right*.

He slanted a glance toward his son. Mickey had been sitting beside him on the sofa for the last half hour. He was staring straight ahead at the set, his expression devoid of any emotion. Spangles was parked at the boy's feet, vainly waiting to be stroked.

Just as Blaine had vainly waited for a glimmer of a smile to appear on Mickey's face at the on-screen antics of an utterly improbable family. Nothing remotely bearing a resemblance to a smile had creased his son's lips.

Had Diane's death completely wiped away Mickey's feelings? No, he wasn't going to accept that. He wasn't certain how, but somehow, he was going to find a way to break through to Mickey.

But not today.

Blaine looked at his watch. It was getting late and was undoubtedly past Mickey's bedtime. He'd never had the boy with him overnight. Even when he'd had the time, Diane hadn't allowed it. They'd call it a night, he decided, and start fresh tomorrow.

"Ready for bed?"

Secretly, he hoped for a protest. Little boys always tried to wangle an extra ten minutes or so. It was inherent in their nature. Bedtime was something to be avoided at all costs, even if you were falling on your face, exhausted.

Mickey rose to his feet. Spangles gained his legs beside him. "Sure."

It suddenly occurred to Blaine that the only spark of emotion he had seen his son display was when the boy had first seen Bridgette. It had gone out almost immediately, but it *had* been there.

That clinched it. If he listened, he could have sworn he heard a cell door clanging shut.

Bridgette was probably the key to unlocking what was boarded up inside of Mickey. Like it or not, he was going to have to put up with the woman for his son's sake.

He didn't like it.

He liked the fact that she was right even less. Right that this subdued manner in which Mickey was dealing with his mother's death wasn't good. Blaine readily admitted that he didn't know much about children, but he knew that Mickey's reaction just wasn't natural. He hadn't seen him shed a single tear, and Jack had told him that the boy had remained dry-eyed at the funeral, as well. Blaine knew Mickey had loved his mother and had been very close to her.

Blaine took Mickey's hand. It curved, small and lifeless, within his. "Want me to tuck you in?"

"If you want to."

A conversation with an apathetic, world-weary old man would have yielded more emotion. For a moment, Blaine thought of just retreating, just giving up. It would have been the easy way out.

But then Bridgette's advice about Mickey's needs echoed through his mind. Harped on it might have been a more apt description. Still, the point was that he wasn't going to get anywhere with Mickey if he gave way and retreated.

He had to find a way to reach him, no matter what it took.

Mickey began to cross to the doorway. Blaine sat down on the coffee table in order to be at eye level with the boy. He placed his hands on Mickey's small shoulders. Mickey turned to look at him. Maybe he could eventually reach him through physical contact.

"No," Blaine contradicted. "What do *you* want? I would like to tuck you in, but I don't want to do anything that might upset you."

Diane had probably tucked him in hundreds of times and Blaine didn't want to remind him of that. God, but this road he found himself on was so hard to navigate. He felt as if he were constantly losing ground.

Blaine searched his son's face, looking to see if anything he was saying was registering.

"Mickey, you're going to have to help me out here. I know I'm your dad." Blaine's mouth curved in a smile. "My name's on your birth certificate, but that doesn't mean I have the skills, the training to do this job right. I've never been the dad of a ten-year-old before. If I mess up, I want you to tell me."

Mickey solemnly nodded his head up and down. "Sure, I'll tell you."

It was like talking to a glass of water, Blaine thought, frustrated. Releasing Mickey, he rose to his feet. "Okay, we'll compromise. Why don't you get ready and I'll look in on you in a few minutes?"

He expected no protest this time and received none. Mickey left the room.

Behind him, credits were running over a scene of the family

they'd been watching for the last half hour. All five people were tangled up in a huge group hug. Blaine pressed the On/Off button. The scene disappeared, folding itself up into a small, round blue dot before vanishing altogether.

He didn't know why he had wasted his time and Mickey's watching the show. Life wasn't a half hour sitcom where problems were neatly resolved in twenty-three minutes—subplots even faster.

But he could wish for that, just this once.

Blaine ran a hand through his hair, upbraiding himself for being foolish. This was going to work out. It was just going to take time. Lots of it.

And some of it, he'd resigned himself, was going to have to be spent in Bridgette's company. Starting at five tomorrow.

He wondered, as he walked down the hall to Mickey's room several minutes later, if she was going to be coming by car or by broom.

The door to Mickey's bedroom stood wide open. Light was flooding out into the hallway. Mickey was afraid of the dark and no paltry night-light adequately held the ghosts and haunts at bay. That was left up to a sixty-watt bulb. And Spangles.

When he looked in, Blaine saw that Mickey was already in bed and apparently asleep. Spangles was stretched out across the foot of the bed like a living black-and-tan accent rug. The German shepherd Blaine had given to his son for his seventh birthday raised his head slightly as Blaine walked in and approached the bed. He was Mickey's dog all the way.

"Mick?" Blaine whispered softly.

Mickey made no response. Long lashes rested like dark crescents against his cheeks. His breathing was steady and rhythmic.

Blaine felt a mixture of disappointment and relief. He'd wanted another opportunity to talk with Mickey, but he had a gnawing feeling that no matter what he said, nothing would be changed. Not yet, at any rate.

He sighed. He was just going to have to be patient. Like a shot that had to be framed just so, things would fall into place, he promised himself. He loved Mickey too much for things not to work out.

Blaine patted the dog's head as Spangles rested his muzzle on his paws. His large brown eyes were trained on Mickey.

"At least he feels he has you," Blaine murmured to the dog. "That's something."

Withdrawing quietly from the room, Blaine didn't see Mickey's eyes opening. Nor did he see the endless well of sadness in them as Mickey turned toward the wall and the photograph of his mother hanging there.

Blaine realized that he had unconsciously been listening for the sound ever since he'd brought Mickey home from school: the sound of a car pulling up in his driveway. He'd been listening for it, anticipating it and dreading it all at the same time. When he finally heard it, Blaine glanced out the window toward the driveway. He was in time to see Bridgette getting out of her silver compact car.

Obviously her broom was in the shop, he thought.

Bracing himself, telling himself that this was for Mickey, Blaine was at the door when the doorbell rang. It sounded oddly like the bell at a boxing arena. Round two, he imagined. Still, if Mickey responded to her, Blaine supposed he could put up with the woman. In small, bite-size doses.

He opened the door and was surprised to note that she appeared somewhat uncomfortable. Now what? Did she have a bomb strapped to her, set to go off within five minutes, and was now wondering how to remain in his company until it detonated?

Bridgette raised her eyes to his. He looked larger than he had yesterday. Or maybe she just felt smaller. Bridgette wasn't in her element.

She'd rehearsed the apology all during the drive over. In

several different versions. No matter how she phrased it, the apology still sounded wrong. It wasn't that apologies were foreign to her. She'd certainly done her share of apologizing in her life, mostly to Gino.

No, it was something else, something more. She just didn't think that the man deserved an apology. In her estimation, he was still a poor excuse for a father, not to mention a wayward husband. The latter was based strictly on Diane's say-so, but she had no reason to doubt her late best friend's allegations. Why would Diane have lied to her?

Still she had promised Nonna to try to make friends with him, or at least to be civil for everyone's sake, especially Mickey's. Jack had confided to her grandmother last night that he felt Mickey was withdrawing into himself even more than he had first thought. She had seen evidence of that for herself firsthand.

And it was obvious that she couldn't be there for Mickey, couldn't help him, if she was busy fighting with his boor of a father.

No, no more recriminations, she upbraided herself just before she'd rung the bell. She'd promised. And, unlike some people, she thought, Blaine's image coming to mind, she never broke a promise. Mickey was far more important to her than any feelings she might—

"Hello."

The single word, warm, sexy and enveloping, put her instantly on her guard. Damn, but he did raise her hackles. And, if she were honest with herself, for more reasons than one.

With all her heart, Bridgette wished that Diane hadn't confided in her to the extent that she had. Listening to the litany of complaints hadn't enabled her to do anything for Diane. Recounting the tales hadn't even been cathartic for her friend. Cataloguing Blaine's faults had been neither cleansing nor helpful to her frame of mind. If anything, it had only depressed Diane.

And it certainly had gone a long way toward tainting her own view of the man, Bridgette thought.

Well, tainted or no, she had a promise to keep.

"Hello," she echoed. Crossing the threshold, she looked about the living room. It was crowded with boxes, just as it had been yesterday. The man obviously moved fast only when it came to his women. "Is Mickey around?"

"In his room. With Spangles," Blaine added in case she wanted to take him to task for some reason about leaving the boy alone. Blaine had no way of second-guessing what she would do or say and he wanted to avoid any scene whatsoever for Mickey's sake.

"Good." She wanted no witnesses to the scene she was about to play out. "I wanted to talk to you."

"Oh, great," he groaned as he shut the door. "Should I go get Jack to act as referee?"

She ignored his sarcastic question, or at least tried to. Bridgette took a deep breath as she turned around to face him.

She turned a little too quickly and her breasts brushed against Blaine. Surprised, he caught her by the shoulders to keep from throwing her off balance. The thought telegraphed itself through his system that touching her, touching any part of her, was a very pleasurable experience. One that, under other circumstances, he would have enjoyed exploring.

As it was, he was afraid of having his hands bitten off. He meant to drop them quickly to his sides, but something inherent within him prevented him from following through. Instead, he slowly slid his palms down the length of her arms before he finally backed away from her.

Bridgette's breath caught in her throat, blocking any words of protest that might have had a chance of emerging. Something hot, stimulating and dangerous sizzled through her. She vehemently denied its existence.

She *couldn't* be reacting to Blaine. She was seeing Roger, and she wasn't the type of woman to be seeing one man and feeling something for another.

Feeling *anything* for another.

So why had she suddenly lost her train of thought, as well as her orientation?

Bridgette cleared her throat while silently damning Blaine O'Connor for ever having been born and subsequently messing up everyone's life. She reminded herself that she still had an apology to deliver, as tasteless as the task was to her.

"About yesterday," she began tentatively, feeling her way around like a soldier on his hands and knees, searching for a way out of an active mine field. "Maybe I came on a little too strong." She didn't believe that she had stated her feelings strongly enough, but saying so to him wouldn't mend any fences.

A smile quirked the corners of Blaine's mouth. "Maybe?"

Bridgette blew out a breath, struggling for composure. This wasn't going to be easy, but what did she expect? As far as this man went, the word *easy* applied only to the women he'd been with.

"Look, I'm trying to apologize to you." Bridgette realized that there was a definite bite to her tone. She lowered her voice just as she saw amusement enter Blaine's eyes. "For Mickey's sake," she added, not wanting him to misunderstand and think that he had anything to do with it. Womanizers, and she'd had her painful experience with one, were wont to misconstrue a lot of things because of their overwhelming egos.

He wondered what had prompted her. It obviously pained her to apologize to him, even though she certainly owed him an apology. She had gone at him like a kamikaze pilot on a death mission.

"All right, for Mickey's sake, I accept." Blaine put out his hand to her. "Truce?"

Bridgette hesitated. Instantly, she was annoyed with herself. And with him. Hesitation was the mark of a person whose convictions were in flux. That in no way described her. She had always forged ahead, afraid of nothing, knowing exactly what her next move was, at least in theory if not in execution.

The last word had her smiling enigmatically at Blaine. Bridgette all but shoved her hand into his, as if a point of honor was at stake.

"Truce."

The handshake was delivered almost like a challenge rather than a settlement. Bridgette wasn't prepared for the electricity that jumped through her veins as his fingers closed on hers. There was no getting away from it. What she was experiencing was a sexual pull. A very strong sexual pull.

How could she be attracted to a man she found detestable? Not to mention Roger…

She didn't want to mention Roger. The man was the furthest thing from her mind as Bridgette watched, fascinated, to see a glint of desire rising in Blaine's light green eyes.

As if she had been scalded, Bridgette pulled her hand away and dropped it to her side.

"Now that that's settled…" she began, having absolutely no idea what she was going to say next.

Nothing was settled, Blaine thought. But a hell of a lot of things were suddenly unsettled.

"I'll find Mickey for you," he volunteered, backing out of the room.

She was barely aware of nodding.

Good, that'll give me time to find myself.

What had come over her? Bridgette touched her cheeks with probing fingertips, as if she could actually feel the color that had crept up to them. She knew they had turned pink because she'd seen it in Blaine's eyes. He'd looked pretty smug about it, too.

She took a deep, cleansing breath, and then another. It didn't help. She refrained from taking a third, afraid that she would hyperventilate just as he returned with Mickey.

Knees suddenly weak, Bridgette sank down on the piano bench.

This was stupid. She was acting like an adolescent schoolgirl. Worse. And she didn't even *like* the man, for heaven's sake. The fact that he seemed to breathe sexuality and had such an effect on her only reinforced what Diane had told her—that Blaine O'Connor had bedroom eyes and slept with every one of his models.

Probably paralyzed them with his eyes like a snake, she thought, fumbling through her portfolio as she looked for the sheets of music she had promised to bring Mickey.

Finding them, she looked up. Mickey was standing beside the piano. Blaine stood behind him. Bridgette forced a wide smile to her lips and received none in return.

"Hi, Mickey."

"Hi."

It was the same lifeless tone she'd heard him use yesterday. Nothing had changed. She had hoped that it might have, but in her heart, she hadn't expected it to.

Bridgette looked up at Blaine, ready to throw a silent accusation his way. But he looked as concerned as she felt. The huge wave of animosity she'd felt rising within her suddenly leveled out and disappeared like the sea at low tide.

Bridgette turned toward Mickey. When he'd first started taking lessons from her less than a year ago, he'd sat on the bench, his thin legs moving to and fro like two pale metronomes. He'd fidgeted like the little boy he was. Now he sat perfectly still. It was almost eerie.

"I brought that new piece I told you about." She placed the single folded sheet onto the music holder. "Want to give it a try?"

He nodded, complying. It was purely a reflexive action, done with no thought, no enthusiasm. No desire. She didn't know if she could bear seeing him like this.

She knew she had no other choice, not if she wanted to help him.

Bridgette moved the music aside. "Or we could talk," she coaxed. She took his hands into hers. "We don't have to play."

Bridgette glanced up at Blaine. Diane had told her that he was incredibly tight with his money. According to her friend, she had to continually threaten him with court action before she received her child support checks. "Don't worry, this is strictly off the meter."

The apology she had tendered only minutes earlier certainly didn't last long. Just what was she implying now? Blaine wondered. What else had Diane told her? Or had Bridgette simply taken an instant dislike to him for some strange personal reason? He wanted to tell her that if she could get Mickey to open up, he'd pay her whatever sum she wanted. But he knew that he couldn't say anything like that in front of Mickey.

He couldn't say a lot of things he wanted to in front of Mickey.

Whatever might be going on between them, Bridgette had come to help his son. Maybe Mickey would do better on a one-to-one basis with her. With an unexpected sting of regret arising from the belief that she was better equipped to help his son than he was, Blaine left the room.

Tension seemed to evaporate the moment Blaine walked out. Finally able to concentrate, Bridgette turned her attention to Mickey. The boy had his fingers poised over the keys.

"We can practice the new piece," he murmured.

Playing could be therapeutic for him. A restoration of routine. Still, she couldn't shake the feeling that they weren't really making progress. She knew Mickey well enough to believe that he was just saying something he thought she wanted to hear.

Helpless, Bridgette began the lesson, hoping that somehow, music would eventually show her the way to bridge the gaps.

Blaine listened from the next room as the halting notes were struck. Slowly they strung themselves into a song that seemed vaguely familiar to him. But he couldn't put a name to it.

Concentrating, he narrowed it down to either "This Land is Your Land" or "Pop Goes the Weasel." The title didn't matter. What did matter was that Mickey was playing.

It was a shaky step forward, he thought, but it was a step. Still, it was going to be a hell of a lot slower process than he had first imagined. He was going to need all the help he could get, including anything that the Wicked Witch of the West could offer.

He frowned to himself as he opened the refrigerator and took out a soda. Apology, huh? He popped the top and took a long sip. It was a lucky thing that she wasn't on the counsel of the UN or war would have broken out a long time ago.

Blaine glanced at the message board above the wall phone in the kitchen. His name leapt out at him. Blaine placed the can on the counter and crossed to the board. Jack's scrawl was barely legible. When had the call come in? he wondered. As a secretary, Jack left something to be desired.

Blaine studied the message for several moments before he finally made sense out of it. The managing editor of one of his magazines had called earlier and wanted a return call. ASAP.

Just what he needed, Blaine thought as he tapped out the numbers on the keypad, more problems. Dealing with Kent Sheffield always meant problems.

He knew what it was about even before he called. It was the assignment, the one dealing with the new line of clothes coming from the hotshot designer in New York. The assignment had been moved around so many times he was seriously thinking of leaving bread crumbs just to locate it.

Undoubtedly, Kent had changed his mind about it.

Again.

Three minutes into the call, Blaine discovered that he was right. Kent *had* changed his mind about the assignment. He wanted it completed. Yesterday.

Blaine tried to siphon the impatience from his voice as he cradled the telephone against his ear. In the background, the strains of music had ceased. He wondered if the lesson was over.

"Look, I can't accommodate you and this floating deadline. If you really want it done, I'm going to need an extension."

"No can do."

Kent's voice grated on his nerves. It always did. Blaine thought he was being rather unreasonable, seeing as how the layout had already been pulled twice in the last three weeks. Maybe he could appeal to the man's sense of decency. Blaine vaguely recalled that Kent had a daughter, though he didn't see her very often since he'd divorced the girl's mother.

And didn't that have a familiar ring to it? he mused.

Blaine didn't like asking for favors, but this wasn't for him. "It's my son, Kent. My ex-wife was killed just over a week ago. I really need to be here for him."

Kent responded with an oath. "So, be there for him next week. I need those photos, O'Connor. Now. The only negatives I want to be handed have celluloid in them, not words. Got it?"

The man was made out of stone. There were threads he wanted to pull together with Mickey. He couldn't do it from New York. "Can't you get someone else?"

"Sure. I could do that."

It was too easy. Blaine knew better than to take the man at his word. He offered his thanks, then waited for the other shoe to fall.

It didn't take long.

"I could also get them on a permanent basis and you could go stand at some freeway entrance with one of those cardboard signs that read, 'Will Work for Food.' How does that sound to you?"

He might have known. "Lousy. You don't have a heart, you know that, Kent?"

A raspy laugh rattled against his ear, followed by a cough that had been twenty years in the making, thanks to a two-pack-a-day habit.

"Sure, I've got a heart, O'Connor. And I've got the medical bills to prove it. Now, don't give me grief, give me a layout. A classy one like I know you're good for. I want you on that plane tomorrow morning, understand? No ifs, ands or buts. Flight 7 out of LAX, 8:00 a.m. Got it?"

Blaine curbed his annoyance. He knew that Sheffield could bad-mouth him, and in this business, success could fly out the window very easily. If he got a reputation as being difficult, his assignments would quickly dry up.

It was an argument he'd used with Diane. It didn't make him any happier now than it did then. Only then, he'd been relieved to leave her and her accusations behind. Now he had a son he felt as if he were abandoning.

"Right. Flight 7, 8:00 a.m." He sighed, scribbling down the information on the message board. "You're a bastard, Kent."

"Yeah, but a successful one. See you."

"See you," Blaine muttered as he hung up.

Maybe he could take Mickey with him, he thought, then dismissed the idea. Dragging around a ten-year-old on a shoot wasn't advisable. Besides, it would be for only two days. That wasn't so long, was it? Most of the time, Mickey was in school. The rest of the time, Jack would be there. And there was always Spangles. He wasn't abandoning Mickey, he was leaving him in good care.

He turned around and saw Bridgette walking into the room. That same judgmental look was in her eyes.

Chapter Four

The image of an angry goddess flashed through Blaine's mind. The only thing that was missing were thunderbolts shooting from either eye to complete the picture. Blaine decided that maybe he'd done one too many theme layouts lately.

He braced himself for the coming storm. "By the look on your face, I'd guess that you have something you're dying to say to me."

"You bet I do." Bridgette glanced over her shoulder to make certain that Mickey was not within hearing range. Satisfied, she crossed to Blaine.

She looked as if she were about to take a swing at him, he thought. "I take it that your former apology is rescinded?"

He was struggling to hold on to his own temper. His need to earn a living warring with his concern for Mickey, Blaine felt as if he were being emotionally pushed to the wall. Right about now, he was dangerously close to overload. The last thing he needed was someone sitting in judgment of him. Just who the hell did she think she was?

Bridgette opened her mouth, but indignation choked off her words. She could only shake her head at her own gullibility. "I was an idiot to think that you actually cared about Mickey."

Good intentions or not, he'd had just about enough of this woman. "Your IQ, or better yet, your common sense," he snapped, "is not in question here. Just what are you condemning me for this time?"

Did he have to ask? "You're going on an assignment, aren't you?"

Blaine suddenly felt as he had been propelled back in time. The need to justify his actions, the probability that nothing he could say would change the look in her eyes, dragged up painful memories. He debated just stalking out and ignoring Bridgette. He owed her no explanations, no excuses.

But she did figure prominently into his son's life and because of that, he was going to have to make a real attempt to get along with her. He tried to look at the situation from her perspective, bearing in mind that all her information had been filtered through Diane.

"Yes, I'm going on assignment." Even though his anger was under control, the look in his eyes dared her to make anything of it.

She didn't leave the challenge unanswered. Standing close to him so that no one else could posssibly overhear, she snarled, "Mickey needs you."

The light scent she wore was impending his thoughts. It seemed to be seeping into his very soul, tangling it up so that it was difficult to hold on to the fact that he wanted to throttle her.

"I'm well aware of that. Mickey also needs to eat and to have a roof over his head, which is why I have to work." Disgusted, afraid that at any moment Mickey might walk in and catch them arguing, Blaine wrapped his fingers around her wrist. Without another word, he led Bridgette to the adjacent family room.

Where did he get off, dragging her around as if she were

some rag doll? She attempted to pull free, but she was no match for him. "What do you think you're doing?"

Blaine spared her one glance over his shoulder as he opened the sliding glass door that led to the backyard. "I'm taking you outside."

That was rather obvious, she thought as she stumbled over the runner. "Why? To throw me out?"

"Don't tempt me."

Blaine released her only after he'd shut the sliding glass door behind them. Being outside gave them a measure of privacy. He figured they were going to need it. One of them was going to blow at any moment.

He turned to face her, still embroiled in a struggle to hold on to the edge of his temper. "You realize I don't owe you an explanation, but here it is. I care about Mickey, I care very much about Mickey—"

She wasn't about to merely stand here and let him think that he could successfully snow her. "So why weren't you ever around?"

It galled him that she sounded so certain of that, based on only what she had been told by one person. "I was," he insisted, louder than he'd intended. "As much as I could be." He saw the disbelief in her eyes. "*More* than Diane wanted to let me."

"*Let* you?" she echoed incredulously. He was lying. Wasn't he? Bridgette lowered her voice to a harsh whisper, afraid that Mickey might hear. "She said that she had to literally beg you to come see Mickey."

"Diane never begged for anything in her life, literally or otherwise. But she did *order* me not to come by. She had the court make it so hard for me to see my son I felt like a trained laboratory rat, stumbling through a labyrinth, trying to reach his goal." His mouth hardened as shards of memories intruded. "She used Mickey as a pawn to punish me for the transgressions she thought I'd committed."

Bridgette looked at him, stunned. How could he say such a thing? But even as her defensiveness for Diane's sake rose, a tiny bit of skepticism began to nibble through her. "Diane loved Mickey."

Why was she so ready to believe that Diane had loved Mickey but he didn't?

"In her own way, yes. But it wasn't a way that was always in his best interests."

If it had been, Diane would have allowed him free access to his son. Blaine felt resentment rising up in his throat, hot and bitter, resentment that Diane had generated over the years. He fought it back. There was no point in allowing himself to be swallowed up by a baser emotion. All that was in the past.

But Bridgette had to be made to see reason. He couldn't continue to listen to groundless accusations, not again.

"The only reason I got to see him at all, or even know about his existence to begin with, was because Jack had the guts to call me and tell me that I was going to be a father. He was the one who called from the hospital to let me know I had a son. He was the one who tried to reason with her." Bitterness twisted his generous mouth. "Diane did everything she could to keep me from Mickey."

It wasn't right. If he was telling her the truth, it wasn't right. There had to be a reason for Diane's actions. Bridgette searched for excuses.

"Well, after the way you treated her—" she began haltingly.

She was heading down the same worn path again. Blaine leveled a cold, penetrating look at her. "Just what did she tell you?"

She wasn't about to stand here and give him a litany of past breeches. That would only feed his ego. "You know what she told me."

His expression didn't change. "For me to know, it would have to have been the truth." He blew out a breath as he slid his hands into his back pockets. "But after having enough accusations hurled at me, I could probably make a good guess." He looked up at the sky, searching for calm. "I slept with every female over the age of eighteen, right?"

He made it sound so ludicrous that she felt guilty for having believed Diane's stories. But then, maybe that was his intent. Vacillating slightly, she nodded. "Something like that."

Blaine shook his head. It never ceased to amaze him that Diane had really believed that. He had loved her once, really, truly loved her. He'd had every intention of loving her to his last breath. She had ruined that for him. For them. He knew he should feel sorry for her, but all he felt was anger.

He did not even try to keep the contempt out of his voice, contempt that Bridgette would be taken in so easily. "Aside from the fact that would make me a walking font of a hell of a lot of communicable diseases, just when was I supposed to be working if I was immersed in this kind of a life-style?"

She wasn't about to be fooled by him. "You tell me."

Leaning a shoulder against the stucco wall, he allowed his eyes to slowly travel up and then down the length of her body. He enjoyed both the view and the effect his scrutiny was having on her. It obviously unsettled her. Good. If Bridgette thought of him as a rutting stud, he could act the part.

For about three seconds.

As soon as he thought of Diane, of what her behavior had cost both of them, not to mention Mickey, his expression changed.

"The answer is, I wouldn't be. I would, however, be in the *Guinness Book of World Records.*" Didn't she understand, yet? "It was Diane's vivid imagination, her rampant insecurity, that killed our marriage. She saw me in bed with everyone, including her sisters."

He allowed himself one long glance at her again. Aside from knowing that it annoyed her, he had to admit that he did like looking at her. She had an almost perfect countenance and yet she didn't have that two-dimensional look to her that so many women with flawless features had. She was exactly the type that Diane would have been jealous of. It seemed rather ironic to him that she had appointed herself Diane's defender.

"If you would have been around while our marriage was still a reality, she would have accused you, too." That seemed to silence her for a moment. The small measure of triumph he felt softened him. "Look, I realize that she had a problem, but it ceased to be mine when we divorced. However, Mickey *is* mine and I want to do everything I can to help him cope with this." He paused, weighing his next words. There was only one way to say it. "You were right."

Bridgette had no idea what he was referring to. "What?"

He'd never liked admitting that he was wrong. He liked admitting that she was right even less. But he wasn't going to get anywhere by butting heads with her.

"I said, you were right." He waved a frustrated hand at her. "And you can gloat if you want to." Given the glimpse of her personality that he'd been privy to, he expected Bridgette to do just that. "Mickey *isn't* handling this. He was never what you could call a happy-go-lucky kid, but right now, he's so stoic, it's scary." Blaine dragged a hand through his hair, lost without any guidelines on the horizon to rescue him. "And I'll be honest, I haven't a clue what to do."

Bridgette hadn't expected this. He wasn't behaving at all the way Diane had said he did. There was no arrogance, no macho postulating. She didn't know which image to believe, but for now, she gave him the benefit of the doubt, even though part of her thought she shouldn't. "You certainly have a way of taking the wind out of a person's sails."

His mouth curved in an amused smile. "Wind, hell, that was a full-fledged gale you had going." He felt himself on the verge of making an ally. Possibly. Blaine surged forward. "Anyway, that so-called truce we struck up, is it only as good as the paper it's written on?"

They'd only shaken hands. His had been warm and oddly protective. "Better."

"Good." He nodded. The sun was glinting in her hair. He framed a shot of her against a white sand dune, then pulled himself back. "Because I need your help."

She could have told him that, but the fact that he admitted it surprised her. And pleased her, although she attempted to keep the latter in perspective.

"Go on."

Asking her a favor was even worse than asking Kent for one. But it had to be done.

He tested the integrity of their new truce. "I do have to go on that shoot. But I'll be back as soon as I can. Two days if I'm lucky." He paused, looking for the right words. "I don't know what your schedule's like."

"Flexible." As a music teacher, she had several elementary schools she visited during the course of each week, as well as two middle schools. But all that was only in the morning hours. The courses she was taking at the university toward her master's took only a bite out of two afternoons a week.

Feeling awkward, something he was unaccustomed to, Blaine pushed on. "Could you stop by and look in on Mickey in the afternoon? Jack's staying here." She probably already knew that, he thought. "But since Mickey seems to respond to you—"

She stopped him. "You don't have to ask. I was going to do it anyway."

Blaine laughed shortly. He already knew her well enough to surmise that the woman was going to do anything she damn well pleased.

"Why doesn't that surprise me?" His smile deepened, allowing just the minor hint of an indentation in his cheek to flicker as he put out his hand to her. "Truce? For real?"

"For real," she agreed warmly.

Bridgette placed her hand in his just as she had done before.

She looked up at him, surprised. That same odd shiver she'd felt earlier was shimmying up her spine. It was creating goose bumps all along her arms even though the day was warm.

He had just spent a great deal of effort convincing her that he wasn't some roving, lascivious tomcat on the constant prowl. It would make absolutely no sense, then, to give in to the sudden urge that wrapped itself around him, capturing him as if he were a mere rabbit that had blindly walked into a snare.

No sense at all, but there were things in this world beyond sense. Emotions were beyond sense. He'd always believed that.

And never more than now.

Blaine released her hand. He slipped his own into her hair, his fingers gently curving around the contours of her face. He saw the wonder in her eyes, could hear the breath caught in her lungs. Or was that his own?

He brought his mouth down to hers. He had absolutely no choice in the matter.

Bridgette stood very still, frozen and yet ignited as she watched his mouth lower to hers. The word *Run* telegraphed itself urgently through her mind. It faded the very next instant, dissolving like a word written in the sand when a wave washed over it.

Just as a wave washed over her. A tidal wave, one that took the rest of her breath away and threatened to drown her.

The attraction to him that she had grudgingly and silently acknowledged flared now like a lit torch held high in the wind. Without thinking, without allowing herself to think, Bridgette wound her arms around Blaine's neck and leaned her body into his. Just for a wondrous instant, she let herself be carried off by her feelings, by the red-hot surge she suddenly felt pumping all through her.

Her head was spinning so badly that she lost all sense as to who and what she was, except totally captivated.

Desire assaulted her body with steel hands. She'd never felt like this before, as if she were swept away, at one with the elements. Her equilibrium off, Bridgette could barely stand. No one had ever dissolved her knees before, not even Matthew, with his silver tongue and his propensity for lies. Certainly not Roger.

Roger.

Bridgette jerked away, startled, ashamed and angry. At Blaine. But most of all, at herself.

She'd tasted sweeter than he had imagined, sweeter than anything he'd ever had. Sweet and yet tantalizing and so drugging that when she pulled away, he had trouble focusing his mind for a moment.

The look of horror on her face blew apart the small fantasy he'd cocooned himself in. Now he'd gone and done it, he thought, chastising himself. She was going to regress and believe every single word Diane had said against him.

But somehow, he couldn't summon up regret for what had just happened. The experience had been too pleasurable to regret. Still, he couldn't let her think that. In her mind, it would only prove everything she'd previously believed.

He did his best to appear contrite. "Look, I didn't mean for that to happen."

Shaken, Bridgette had to drag air back into her lugs. She fervently wished that her heart would stop emulating a disco beat and settle down in her chest where it belonged.

Wow.

Bridgette looked at him and was surprised that he wasn't gloating. He had every right to. Maybe he wasn't as bad as Diane had said after all. She had no idea whom to believe— someone she had known for years, or a man who should have come with a disclaimer written across his lips: Lethal. Could Be Hazardous To Your Health.

She swallowed before she trusted her voice. "That makes two of us."

Well, at least she wasn't clawing and spitting at him like a cornered alley cat. That was something, Blaine thought.

The interest that just had been aroused refused to remain in the shadows. "Would it negate everything I just said if I told you I was attracted to you?"

The indignation that she wanted to cloak herself in refused to come. "It does put it on pretty shaky foundations." Her response lacked conviction.

"It shouldn't." Because he wanted to touch her just once more, he lightly slid his fingers along her throat. He saw the pulse there jump. Good, at least the response hadn't been one-sided. Not that he really believed it could be after what he had just experienced. Bridgette had kissed him back. Passionately. Jack's description of Bridgette echoed in his mind. Good old Jack, right again. "I'm not seeing anyone right now."

That didn't make what just happened right. Bridgette looked down at the ground. "I am."

Blaine stared at her. He suddenly felt as if a weight had just dropped on his chest. A heavy one. He couldn't quite explain why he felt so disappointed, he just did. "What?"

"I'm seeing someone," she clarified. "A very nice someone." Guilt washed over her, sticky and ensnaring like a spider's web. "I shouldn't have let you kiss me. I'm sorry."

It didn't seem nearly adequate enough. For any of them— least of all, for Roger. Roger, who was stability personified. Roger, who would have never done what she just did.

Blaine saw that she was struggling with her conscience. "We just kissed, Bridgette. You didn't volunteer to become a card-carrying, strolling hostess of the evening." She glared at him and in an odd way, it made him feel that she was coming around. "Would it make you feel any better to blame me for this?"

It would make her feel infinitely better to shrug off the blame for this. "Yes."

He lifted a shoulder and then let it drop, unfazed. "Then go ahead. Blame me." She looked at him sharply. Grinning, he continued. "You've blamed me for everything else, you might as well add this to the list."

Much as she would have wanted to, she couldn't. Not in good conscience, at any rate. Blaine hadn't grabbed her and pulled her into his lair, or dragged her into the bushes. He had kissed her right here out in the open, a stone's throw away from his former father-in-law and his son. And she had let him. That made her as guilty as he. Maybe more because she'd responded.

It was the response that bothered Bridgette. A great deal.

She looked at him suspiciously. "Why are you being nice?" She had all but ripped off his head at their first meeting. Why was Blaine acting so chivalrous all of a sudden?

Confusion, he decided, looked good on her. He began to frame yet another shot in his mind before he realized what he was doing. Blaine shoved his hands into his pockets once again, more to keep from touching her than for any other reason. "Did it ever occur to you that it might be my nature?"

"No."

At least she was honest, he thought, suppressing a smile. Unconsciously running the very tip of his tongue over his lower lip, he could still taste her. And knew that he wanted to again.

"Well, let it occur to you. Because it happens to be true." He sighed, looked toward the sliding door and the room within. "Now if you'll excuse me, I still have a little boy to talk to."

She knew this wasn't going to be easy, for either of them. "I'll come with you," she volunteered, following Blaine inside.

Surprised, he regarded her in silence for a moment, then nodded. "Thanks."

An emotion Bridgette couldn't put a name to passed through Mickey's eyes when Blaine told the little boy he had to go away. It was a mixture of sadness and a deadness that frightened her.

Bridgette was quick to interject, "But your father will be back in two days and I'll come by to see you after school." She placed a comforting hand over his. "Maybe we could even go out to the movies with your grandfather. Would you like that?"

It appeared as if it were all one and the same to him. "You don't have to."

She exchanged a look with Blaine. "No, but I really want to."

"Okay." Mickey returned to his video game, blocking both of them out.

For the first time, Blaine was grateful that Bridgette had barged her way into this. He had someone else to share his fear with.

"I really appreciate this," Blaine told her as he walked her to her car. It occurred to him that several hours ago, he would have never thought he'd hear himself say that. Several hours ago, he hadn't seen himself kissing her, either.

She opened the passenger side and tossed in her portfolio. It bounced off the seat and wedged itself on the floor. Bridgette rounded the hood before looking toward Blaine.

She felt better with a barrier between them. "I said you don't have to thank me. I love Mickey. It's no hardship for me to come over to see him."

Blaine cut the distance between them. "About before—"

She didn't want to discuss it. She didn't want to feel the nettles of guilt sting her again.

"Why don't we forget it?" she suggested a bit too quickly.

But Blaine shook his head. "I'm not sure I can." He saw a wariness enter her eyes. "This other person you're seeing, is it serious?"

It was from Roger's standpoint. She'd believed it was from hers, as well. Or thought she did before today. Roger was steady, dependable. A rock. He served as an anchor to her more volatile personality. And if there were times that the anchor weighed just a little too heavily, well, he had a lot of virtues that offset that. She had had passion in her life once—white lightning, blinding passion—and had paid a price for it. The man she had gone with before Roger was everything that Blaine

O'Connor was. Handsome, charming, smooth. And married. The last was a fact he'd forgotten to tell her. She'd discovered it by accident, and it had taken her a long time to get over it. Commiserating with Diane had helped. It had also taught her to be distrustful of smooth, good-looking men.

"He's asked me to marry him."

"And you said yes?"

She wished he'd stop looking at her as if he had answers that she hadn't formed, yet. "I said I'd think it over."

That was all he wanted to know. It corroborated what he had felt in her kiss. "Then it's not serious."

Of all the cocky, self-centered, egotistical— "Just how do you figure that?"

"Easy." The smile on his face slivered up and down her body like a warm caress. "If it was serious, you would have said yes right away." Blaine looked at her knowingly. "You're that kind of a person."

She didn't like being pigeonholed. "How do you know what kind of a person I am?"

Some things were intuitive. In this case, he'd had a little more input. "Jack told me."

Just what was it that Nonna was telling Jack? Bridgette knew that Nonna liked Roger, but there was a lack of enthusiasm in her grandmother's face when she spoke about Bridgette's possible future with the man. In any event, Blaine had no right to draw conclusions about something that was none of his business.

"Hearsay?"

Blaine laughed. There was a very pronounced note of triumph in the sound. "I believe there's an old saying about the pot calling the kettle black that might apply right about now."

Bridgette had the good grace to flush. He had her there. And she didn't like it. "Is there a saying about the pot hitting the kettle?"

He found that feisty look in her eyes appealing now that it was stripped of daggers. "Not that I'm aware of."

Bridgette got into her car and shut the door. "I might just start a precedent." She leaned out the window and looked up at him, growing serious. "It wouldn't hurt for you to call Mickey when you land in New York."

It wasn't a bad suggestion. "I hadn't thought of that," he admitted.

Living the kind of life he did, Blaine wasn't accustomed to having to check on, or in, with anyone. There were a lot of things he was going to have to get used to, he thought, if he was going to make this father thing work.

"I didn't think so." Bridgette turned on the ignition. "Have a good flight, O'Connor. And don't get lost."

Blaine stepped aside and watched as she pulled away. "I think I already have," he murmured to himself.

Blaine always enjoyed shoots. He thought of them as mini-adventures that took him to a variety of interesting places and thrust him into the company of a myriad of people, some pleasant, some not. But all in all, he found it an exhilarating way to make a living.

This zest for his work allowed him to always give one hundred percent and resulted in his talent being in demand. Concentration was never a problem. It just came to him, as naturally as breathing.

It didn't this time. This time, it was an effort.

Unlike all the other shoots he'd been on, when he'd leave all the things that were going wrong in his life behind him, this time he took the baggage with him. Part and parcel.

He worried about Mickey, about the effect his sudden departure—so quick on the heels of Diane's death—might have on his son. He had called Mickey from his hotel room as soon as he'd checked in. The boy had sounded even more morose.

Guilt nibbled at Blaine as he'd hung up and continued to take out small sections of him all through the shoot.

This was all Bridgette's doing. It was her fault he felt so guilty. Up until now, he'd only been worried, but not guilty.

It was also her fault that he felt so damn restless. Unsettled, like a photograph that had no focal point. All her fault.

Away from her, away from the flashing eyes and the enticing scent that wafted under his skin, he could think a little more clearly. Just what the hell did he think he was doing, entertaining any sort of romantic notions about a harpy?

Granted, she'd sheathed her claws that last time but hadn't he had enough experience with Diane to know how quick those claws could come out? The very last thing he needed in his life right now was to get involved with a hot-blooded, razor-tongued, demanding woman.

So, why was he thinking about her at all?

Why had he envisioned her in every shot he'd taken when there was an entire army of supple, smooth-skinned models parading around between takes in less than a whisper of covering?

He was a normal, healthy male, but he was completely oblivious to the women around him, other than seeing them as part of a whole, the whole being the layout. He'd been at this too long to view the models in any sort of romantic sense. That was strictly reserved for wet-behind-the-ears novices newly introduced to the banquet.

It wasn't so much that he had feasted as that he had become anesthetized to it. Besides, he didn't believe in mixing business with pleasure.

He'd tried to explain all this to Diane, but it had been absolutely to no avail. She hadn't believed that he wasn't interested in an eight-by-ten glossy, but in a woman of substance. Or at least he had been. Once.

Right now, all he wanted was for Mickey to be Mickey again.

And yet, there was no getting away from the fact that one small, loquacious woman had been consistently firing up his imagination and consequently his blood for the last two days.

He couldn't wait to get on that plane and fly home so that he could go about the business of getting her out of his system. The best way to do that, he knew, was to immerse himself in her faults.

As Blaine raised his camera again, ready to take another roll of film of the waiflike seventeen-year-old who was the newest rage splashed across all the leading magazine covers, he felt confident that Bridgette would give him every opportunity to do so.

Chapter Five

It had been one hell of a return trip. The flight Blaine was on had been delayed. Twice. It had something to do with a last-minute verification of a fuel line. All Blaine knew was that it added three hours to his ordeal.

To compound the never-ending joys of traveling, there was an unscheduled layover in Dallas. An unexpected storm front had emerged from nowhere in the west. The pilot hadn't wanted to risk flying directly through it. It wasn't a decision Blaine could fault him for. The delay, however, was another matter.

His plane finally arrived at LAX at approximately the same time as several other flights. The baggage claim area was a mob scene. It had taken him nearly an hour to collect all his equipment. By the time Blaine had deposited it and himself into a cab, he was tired, hungry and not in the best of moods. All he wanted to do was crawl into bed and get a few hours' sleep.

As the cab inched through the thick rush-hour traffic from LAX to Orange County, Blaine fervently hoped that there would be no emergencies to face when he arrived home. He wasn't up to it.

When the taxi dropped him off at his door two hours later, Blaine recognized Bridgette's car in the driveway. So much for getting his wish. If ever there was an emergency in progress, it was her.

He sincerely hoped that she was feeling unaggressive tonight. He had no energy to verbally spar with her and defend himself.

Mixed feelings wafted through him as he placed money in the driver's outstretched hand. The cab backed up as Blaine picked up his equipment and suitcase and turned toward the house. He walked to the front door like a man on his way to the gladiator arena.

Blaine dug into his pocket for his house key. It took him a minute before he managed to get it into the lock and finally open the door.

It didn't look like the same house.

For one thing, the haphazardly scattered piles of boxes were gone. Not a single one remained within the neatly arranged room. It looked like the average living room, with some of his old furniture trying to get acquainted and meld with some of Diane's that he had decided to keep. He'd done it for Mickey's sake. He'd never really cared for her taste.

Like a homing pigeon, he made for his favorite chair, the one he'd had reupholstered twice. Reaching it, he sank down, letting the familiar shape cocoon him.

Only then did Blaine smile at the scene he'd walked into.

Bridgette was on the floor, playing a board game with Mickey. Laughing over a move that cost her a fair amount of tiny real estate, Bridgette glanced up at Blaine. There was sheer pleasure in her face and he wanted to think that some of it was there because he'd just returned, though he knew that was probably reaching. She was wearing jeans that adhered to her like a second skin and a pink, sleeveless body blouse that made him aware of how very female she was. Sitting there cross-legged on his floor, Bridgette looked more inviting than a toasty fire on a cold day.

Blaine had an overwhelming urge to warm himself.

"Hi." For one second, she felt almost shy in the face of his appraising glance. Brushing off her hands, Bridgette rose to her feet. "You're late."

This time there was no accusation in her words, only an observation, mingled with what sounded like a trace of relief. He looked around and wondered where Jack was, although, for the moment, he hadn't the energy to get up and look for the man.

"The elements and several airplane mechanics conspired against me." He looked at his son, who was carefully counting out play money before awarding it to himself. "Hi, Mickey, how are you doing?"

Was it his imagination, or was there a small spark of something in his son's eyes? A small spark that indicated a little boy still lived inside there.

"Hi." Mickey glanced toward Bridgette. "I'm beating her," he announced with a sliver of pride.

"Badly," Bridgette agreed. It was getting late and she had to go home to get ready for her date. "Which means I'm going to quit. You know how I hate to lose." She winked at Mickey, refraining from tousling his hair. One tiny milestone at a time. Getting him to play a game with her was triumph enough for one day.

Mickey began to methodically put away the game pieces into the box. He spared a glance at his father. "I always win."

And she probably let him, Blaine thought. Nice trick. "Hang on to that feeling." He looked at Bridgette. "Men don't get to do that much when they get older."

Since she was standing, he rose to his feet, feeling perhaps a little less weary than before. The way she filled out her body blouse had a lot to do with that. He gestured around the room.

"What happened to all the boxes?" He'd told Jack not to bother with them until he returned. Jack didn't strike him as the type who wanted to take on unpacking another man's things on his own.

"I put them away," she answered matter-of-factly. She should be on her way, Bridgette thought. Why was she lingering here like this, exchanging inane conversation? Stalling. She was afraid of the answer.

She certainly did make herself at home, he thought. "Full?"

Bridgette shook her head. "No, they were empty. I took the liberty of unpacking and arranging things for you." And had done a pretty good job of it, too, she thought. If Blaine was anything like Gino, the boxes would have remained where they were for six months, if not longer. Blaine struck her as a procrastinator. Mickey needed order and permanency in his life, not an obstacle course.

Blaine frowned slightly. *Liberty* was the word for it, all right. "But you don't know where I want things," he protested.

She shrugged nonchalantly. "I guessed." She'd commandeered Jack and Mickey, turning it into a family project. "Mickey helped," she added with a smile, curtailing any complaint Blaine might be tempted to raise about his belongings being tampered with.

Because she seemed to barge in as if she belonged, Blaine assumed that she was here for the evening. When she picked up her purse, he knew he'd miscalculated. "Aren't you staying for dinner?" And hopefully cooking it, he added silently.

She shook her head. "I have a date."

"With Roger?"

She raised her chin, feeling it necessary to defend the absent man. "Yes. Roger and I are doubling with my grandmother and Jack." She'd arranged it last night when Roger had called. She had felt the need for company. Maybe it was guilt over the kiss, but she hadn't wanted to face Roger alone.

"Jack and your grandmother," Blaine repeated as if saying it aloud helped him absorb the information. At least she wasn't going to be alone with the guy. "So, it'll be a nice, quiet date."

Jack walked into the room at that moment. He thought he'd heard Blaine's voice.

"Welcome home, son." He was adjusting his tie and there was a gleam in his eye. He looked almost dapper. "And I wouldn't count on it being a quiet date if I were you. We're going dancing." A smug smile creased his mouth. "Don't wait up."

She was going dancing. This Roger character was going to be holding her. Close. Why that would annoy him wasn't something Blaine felt up to exploring.

Blaine looked at Mickey. "So, it looks like it's just you and me, Mickey." Mickey placed the box on the coffee table and nodded silently. "Got any ideas?"

In reply, Mickey merely shook his head.

Bridgette had every intention of leaving. She still had to change for dinner. But the look on Mickey's face froze her in place. She couldn't just leave him like this.

"Mickey, didn't you mention the other day that you'd like to go to Squirrely's?"

"Squirrely's?" Blaine repeated, wincing. The very name didn't sound promising.

There was so much he had to learn, she thought. Squirrely's was a favorite place for the under-fourteen set. "It's not far from here. They serve pizza and they have all-you-can-eat buffets."

Blaine could just imagine what those buffets were comprised of.

"And arcade games for kids of all ages," Bridgette added. She turned toward Mickey. "What do you say, Mickey? It'll be fun, and I think your dad needs a little fun in his life."

She glanced toward Blaine and he could have sworn there was pure mischief in her eyes. He had a feeling that he and his tired body were going to hate Squirrely's.

Mickey glanced at his dog. "Can Spangles come, too?"

It was the first time he'd shown any outward interest in the dog since the funeral. Bridgette felt like shouting for joy.

"Pizza's not good for dogs, sweetie." She bent down, her hands on his shoulders. "He'll understand," she promised. Bridgette looked over toward Blaine.

He realized what was expected of him and mentally picked up the baton she'd silently passed him.

Getting up, Blaine crossed to Mickey. "So, how about it, Mickey? Want to show your dad how to have a good time?"

Mickey's expression was dubious, but at least it was a change from the indifferent one he'd worn. "Yeah, I guess so."

Blaine's response was warm, encouraging. "Knew I could count on you."

Mickey slanted a look at Bridgette. "Can Bridgette come, too?"

I can definitely count on you, Blaine thought.

He pulled his lips into a solemn expression. "Bridgette has a date." But even as he said it, he looked at her expectantly.

Trust Blaine not to play fair. "I really can't, Mickey. I…"

Her voice trailed off helplessly. Bridgette looked down at the boy's face and knew she was lost. Though he wasn't articulating it, he was asking something of her. How could she refuse?

She hesitated, wavering. She didn't appreciate the look in Blaine's eyes. The beast was enjoying this, damn him.

"Why don't you go with them?" Jack urged. "I'm sure Roger'll understand. Besides," he chuckled, "Sophia and I are old enough to go out alone."

Bridgette was torn. It wasn't fair to treat Roger in a cavalier manner. He didn't deserve it. But she didn't want to turn Mickey down, either.

The fact that Blaine would be along only made things that much more difficult.

She glanced at her watch. Roger would just be getting home now. Trapped in what felt like a no-win situation, she tried to ease her conscience. After all, it was only dinner she was canceling. It wasn't as if they'd made plans to see a play or something along those lines. They could go out tomorrow night, instead.

"All right." She addressed her answer to Mickey, then looked at Blaine as an afterthought. "I need to use your telephone."

Bridgette saw Jack and Blaine exchanged glances as she turned to leave the living room. If there was ever such a thing as a visual high five, Bridgette knew she'd just witnessed it.

The man was definitely too smug for his own good.

"This is strictly for Mickey's sake," she tossed over her shoulder as she walked out.

"Never thought anything else." Amusement echoed in Blaine's voice.

The hell he didn't, she thought. He probably thought that she'd done nothing but think about him since he'd left. That just because he'd kissed her, she was holding her breath until he returned. Nothing could be further from the truth. So she was attracted to him. It meant nothing. She was attracted to Mel Gibson, and that wasn't going to lead anywhere, either.

Why did she even feel the need to make all these excuses to herself?

Bridgette gritted her teeth and fairly punched out the numbers on the keypad. The telephone on the other end rang four times. She was preparing herself to talk to the answering machine, relieved that she wouldn't have to speak to Roger directly, when he finally picked up.

"Hello?"

She could feel the muscles in her stomach tightening. "Roger, it's Bridgette."

"Bridgette."

The concern in his voice was instantaneous. It made her feel guilty, even though she told herself that she had nothing to feel guilty about. *Yet.* The word whispered along her mind like a promise.

"What's wrong?"

"Nothing's wrong, Roger." She caught herself wrapping the cord around her fingers and stopped. "But I have to break our date for tonight." The silence that greeted her words had her hurrying to add, "Something's come up. Mickey needs me."

"Is he hurt?"

"No."

"Then I don't understand."

No, she didn't suppose that he would. Roger didn't really care for children. They made him nervous. And he seemed to have completely blanked his own childhood from his mind. She sincerely hoped that would change once they had children of their own.

"He wants me to take him out to a restaurant."

Roger sighed rather loudly, clearly confused. "And I want to take you out to a restaurant. We seem to have a conflict here, don't we?"

She could almost visualize Roger, his handsome, patrician face somber, his brows drawn together, forming a line between them. Bridgette felt impatience drumming through her as she tried to make him understand. "Roger, he's a little boy—"

"Yes," Roger readily conceded. "But he's not *your* little boy."

Roger had been understanding until this point. Maybe he had thought he was indulging her, Bridgette suddenly realized. But it wasn't a game or a hobby she was dealing with that needed indulgence. This was a child, a child she was close to. A child who, in his own way, brought back the echoes of the past to her.

"I can't ignore the fact that he's hurting just because he's not my flesh and blood. I'm his godmother. Diane was my friend."

"And I'm the man you're seeing. Exclusively. That's supposed to count for something."

Bridgette dragged her hand through her hair, restless. It annoyed her that Roger was behaving so heartlessly. Had she misjudged him after all? She'd thought that he was a kind man. She didn't like what she was seeing emerge.

"It does." But she said the words with no feeling.

"Good, then I'll see you in an hour."

Bridgette drew herself up. She didn't like being ordered

around, no matter how politely it might have been phrased. "No, you won't."

There was a pause on the other end of the line. Then Roger asked in a very confused voice, "Am I competing with this child?"

Yes, it was beginning to be clear that she'd been wrong about this man, this rock she thought she'd build her foundation on, just as she had been wrong about Matthew before him.

It didn't say much for her judgment in men, she thought, glancing toward the other room, where Blaine was.

"No, Roger, you're competing with yourself. And you're losing."

"You're not making any sense."

It was something that he habitually accused her of. Sense in Roger's world was very logical, very bloodless. She was beginning to feel that she had no place in his orderly life. Not if it was so narrow in scope.

"Maybe not," she agreed tersely. "I'll see you tomorrow, Roger." Bridgette was about to hang up when she paused. Maybe she was letting her temper get the better of her. Maybe she was looking to pick a fight with Roger because Blaine had rattled her cage so much the other day. "I promise I'll make it up to you."

"All right." Roger sounded resigned. "I'll see you tomorrow."

"Tomorrow," Bridgette echoed, hanging up.

Biting her lip, she turned around. Blaine was standing in the doorway. She should have known. The back of her neck had been itchy, as if someone were watching her. And listening.

"Eavesdropping?"

He crossed to the refrigerator. "Coming in for a soda," he said innocently. He took out a can and popped the top. A small spray of fizz shot out over his hand. He hardly noticed. His attention was on Bridgette. "So, how are you going to make it up to him?"

She could see by the look in his eyes how he *thought* she was going to make it up to Roger. "That is none of your business."

He shrugged nonchalantly, studying her over his can as he took another sip. "Well, it is in a way, seeing as how you canceled your date because of me."

The man had gall, she'd give him that. "Because of Mickey."

Her correction didn't faze him. "He's my son, so it makes it because of me by proxy."

Bridgette moved past him. She refused to continue with this conversation. "Don't let it worry you."

In one swift movement, he set down the can on the counter and cornered Bridgette against the wall. "I missed you." The words he uttered were soft, low and all the more dangerous for it.

All she had to do was push him away. Just one little push. Or one big one, which was what he deserved. She remained immobile. All of her but her heart, which insisted on doing double time. "Don't cloud this issue up for me, O'Connor."

It had been a long time since he had felt this attracted to a woman. A very long time. The fact that he knew it was mutual and that she was resisting made it that much more enticing. "You know, I have a first name."

She brazened it out. "Most people do."

His son was a room away, waiting. But Blaine couldn't resist lingering just a moment longer. He lightly ran the back of his hand along her cheek. He saw something akin to desire glint, just for a moment, in her eyes. It was enough. For now. He made himself a promise to explore that desire, and soon.

"I'd really like you to use it."

If he didn't stop tying her stomach into knots like this, she was going to have to do something drastic to make him. "Why?"

A smile slowly curled its way along his lips. "Call it a crazy whim." His breath caressed her, just as his hand had. "Say it. Say my name."

She rolled her eyes and tried to look as if she were bored by all this. "Blaine."

He was right. The sound of his name on her tongue wove

its way along his skin like a warm, seductive desert breeze. "Very good."

He was going to kiss her, she suddenly realized. And she wanted him to.

This wasn't good.

With a quick thrust, she pushed him away. "Mickey's waiting."

Trying to look as if she weren't fleeing, she turned and left the room.

"Squirrely's," Blaine repeated with a shake of his head. "I can't wait."

It wasn't nearly as bad as Blaine had anticipated. As a matter of fact, after he became acclimatized to the din and the crowd, he actually found himself enjoying it. It was refreshing to be in the midst of such innocence, he mused, looking around. This, he thought, was what he'd imagined life was going to be like when he married Diane. Simple. Sweet and uncomplicated.

If he wasn't careful, he thought, working his way through another slice of pizza, he was going to talk himself into something. Something that more than likely wasn't going to happen.

He didn't believe in simple dreams anymore.

"You know," he said, raising his voice to be heard, "the food here isn't half bad."

She laughed. By her count, Blaine had consumed six pieces of pizza to her two. Mickey was nibbling on the pepperoni on his third and looked pretty full. "How many would you have eaten if it was good?"

"I was hungry," Blaine protested, finishing the piece in his hand. Now that the edge was off his hunger, he had to admit that he'd had better. "I can't eat at cloud level, suspended in a little silver box."

Bridgette looked at him, surprised at what he was telling her. "Are you afraid of flying?"

He glanced at Mickey. Was it good for a son to think his father was afraid of something? He'd never had to wrestle with that at Mickey's age. His father had been a giant of a man who always behaved as if he were afraid of nothing.

"Not afraid," Blaine corrected. "Let's just say a little leery."

He was searching for euphemisms, she thought. "But you do it all the time."

Blaine shrugged, reaching for the tall, complimentary pitcher of soda that was included with the order of an extra-large pizza. He refilled Bridgette's glass and topped off Mickey's before pouring some into his own. "That doesn't mean I have to like it."

So he had fears. Who would have thought it? She realized that she rather liked that. It made him more human. "I've heard it's safer than driving."

He laughed. He'd heard that one a dozen times if not more, but it still didn't make him feel any better about it.

"If something goes wrong with the car, you can always get out and walk away from it. That isn't advisable in a plane." He sat his amber glass down and turned to his son. "So, Mickey, now that we've filled up, want to play one of those games?"

Mickey looked toward the arcade. There was no one playing his favorite game. "Well—"

Bridgette saw the inch, grabbed it and ran a mile with it. "Sure he does." She smiled encouragingly at Mickey. "Did you know that his name's on the Masters of the World honor roll? He ran up over a million points in one game." Bridgette remembered standing beside Mickey, feeding him quarters until he'd gotten the hang of the game.

"I was lucky," Mickey mumbled, but there was just the smallest hint of pride in his voice when he said it.

"Why don't you show your father how it's done?" Bridgette urged.

Mickey hesitated, then finally slid off the bench. Blaine flashed Bridgette a grateful look.

"Watch him," she instructed. "You might learn something."

Blaine looked at her significantly. "I think I'm learning something already."

Bridgette had no idea what he was referring to, but she still felt as if she'd been somehow exposed.

She pushed the tray aside and pick up her glass, sipping slowly. What in the world was she doing here, anyway? she wondered.

The answer was simple. And complex. She was enjoying herself. She might have initially come here for Mickey's sake but she was enjoying herself for a number of reasons. More than she wanted to. And some of that had to do with Blaine.

Bridgette sighed as she looked down at the glass in her hand and wished fleetingly for something a little stronger. She wasn't supposed to like him. She didn't *want* to like him. After all, her loyalty lay with Diane.

But, loyalty, or not, Blaine was seeping in, like water through a fissure on a stone.

She shook her head as she continued to sip her flat soda. Things were getting complicated. She watched Mickey as he stood before the flashing, whirling lights. Blaine was beside him, cheering him on. As Mickey scored another hit, Blaine looked over his shoulder at her.

Yes, things were definitely getting very, very complicated.

They stayed at Squirrely's for over two hours. By the time they returned home, Mickey had fallen asleep in the back seat, exhausted. He hadn't been sleeping well since his mother's death. The combination of sleeplessness and excitement had knocked him out.

Blaine parked his car beside Bridgette's, not bothering with the garage door opener. Getting out, he opened the rear passenger door and then stood, debating whether or not to wake Mickey.

Bridgette made his mind up for him. "Why don't you just carry him in?"

He nodded and slowly drew the boy out. Mickey was still clutching the tickets he'd won in exchange for racking up points in the arcade game. Connected, they trailed after him like a long purple streamer.

"I think he had a good time," Blaine confided softly to Bridgette, then smiled at her over his son's head. "Thanks."

Since he had his arms full of Mickey, she took the key out of Blaine's hand and unlocked the front door. Opening it, she waited for him to step through before following. Spangles was at their side immediately, prancing from foot to foot as he greeted them. He fell into step beside Blaine.

"You were the one he played with." She shut the door behind her.

Blaine waited for her to follow before he headed toward Mickey's room. "Yes, but you were the one who encouraged him."

"Stop." She held up her hand before pulling back the cover on Mickey's bed. "The next thing you know, we're going to like each other."

Blaine placed Mickey on the bed. He raised his eyes toward Bridgette. "Don't we? At least a little?"

She wished he wouldn't look at her like that. It made her forget things, like the fact that she was engaged. Sort of. "I—"

He grinned. She looked flustered. "For one thing, you weren't shooting daggers at me this time. I know. I checked for holes in the boys' room."

Mechanically, she slipped Mickey's sneakers off, then his socks. "I never shot daggers at you," she insisted in a loud whisper.

Blaine arched a skeptical brow as he drew the covers over his sleeping son. "You weren't on the receiving end of those looks."

Bridgette ignored the sarcasm and nodded toward Mickey. "Aren't you going to take his clothes off and put on his pajamas?"

He shrugged, moving away from the bed. Spangles was already draping himself over the comforter. "I figure he needs to sleep more than he needs to be correctly attired."

She smiled as she stepped out into the hallway. "You're learning."

"Yeah." Blaine slipped his arm around her shoulders. "A lot of things."

Very deliberately, she shrugged off his arm. "Not nearly as much as you think."

Undaunted, Blaine took her hand as they walked toward the living room again. "Know what I think? I think I'm learning more than you want me to."

He was treading a little closer to the truth than she wanted him to. "I know it's English, because the words sound familiar, but—"

He stopped and forced her to turn toward him. "No buts, Bridgette. No arguing, no nothing. Just shut up for a minute." His eyes washed over her face and lingered on her lips. "It's hard to kiss a moving target."

The wall was at her back and he was very definitely at her front. Bridgette felt her breath backing up again as anticipation did a two-step through her body. "Maybe that's the idea."

Blaine slowly moved his head from side to side. "A bad one. Take it from me." He drew her into his arms. "A very bad one. I've been waiting to do this for two days."

She unconsciously licked her lips. The flash of desire in his eyes told her she'd made a tactical mistake.

"Roger…" she began, a protest hovering on her lips.

What she wanted to say was that Roger wouldn't like her kissing someone else.

She never got the chance.

"—Isn't here. And I am."

Watching her eyes, Blaine brought his mouth down to hers.

Chapter Six

It was as if she had been holding her breath for the last two days and was now allowed to exhale. The feeling that surged through Bridgette the moment Blaine's lips met hers was exhilarating beyond anything she could imagine.

The kiss was hot, wanting, passionate. Something within her sprang up to meet it, to meet the silent challenge of his mouth. To meet it and to be undone by it at the same moment.

But she went down fighting.

Like a magnet and an iron filing that had been released at the same moment, they clung to each other, giving, taking, and losing their own identities in the process.

Cleaving to him, Bridgette shut off the little voice within her head that whispered no. Shut off everything except for the wealth of stellar feelings encompassing her.

It made absolutely no sense, Blaine thought, when there were so many women around him who would be more than accommodating if he would show the slightest signs of interest, why he should find this one contrary creature so attractive. So damn compelling.

And yet there was no other woman he wanted to kiss, no other woman he wanted to hold.

No other woman he wanted to make love with.

Blaine knew the signs and he didn't like them. He didn't like being held prisoner like this. He didn't like not having a say in whom he cared for.

It made no difference.

Later, he'd think about this later.

His mouth slanted over hers as he tried to satisfy himself and succeeded only in arousing his hunger further. All he wanted right now was to savor the moment. To feel her skin flow like shimmering mercury through his fingers.

To hold her and pretend that there weren't consequences to pay for feeling this way. If only for a little while, he could pretend that she was soft-spoken and wonderful. And that relationships really did have a snowball's chance in hell of succeeding.

Bridgette felt as if she were on fire, being consumed by it. She felt helpless and all-powerful at the same moment. None of it made any sense. There was such a litany of charges against Blaine in her mind, charges she still hadn't satisfactorily put to rest. So why did she want to sell her very soul for this moment to go on?

She didn't even like him.

Did she?

Her heart was beating so fast, so hard, she thought her chest was quaking. Wanting to push him away, she only managed to tangle her hands in his hair. She was so confused!

With an effort that lacked conviction, Bridgette tried to pull away. "I have to go home," she breathed against his mouth.

"Later," Blaine whispered against her temple as he pressed a kiss there. His mouth skimmed across her forehead, leaving her trembling in his wake. "Much later."

Her knees were melting like butter on a hot piece of toast. Bridgette held on to his shirt front.

Blaine's mouth grazed the point of her chin. Bridgette tilted her head back, eager to absorb the heated sensations the very contact created. She realized that she was arching into him, into the kiss. Into a very dangerous situation.

"Now," she breathed with her last shred of energy.

"Now," Blaine echoed.

The next moment he lifted her into his arms, more than ready to comply with her entreaty. He wanted to make love with her so much that it bordered on pain.

Suddenly there was no floor beneath her, and Bridgette's eyes flew open. She looked at him, startled.

"No, I meant now," she repeated vainly. "I have to go home now, not—" Flustered, she could only cling to the word. *"Now."*

A bittersweet smile traced his lips as he finally understood her meaning. Blaine knew it would take very little to convince her to stay the night, to share his bed and his passion. He could see it all there in her eyes. And he ached for her the way he hadn't ached for a woman in a very long time.

But he didn't want to convince her. He wanted her to know that it was what she wanted. He wanted her to be sure, not to be coerced.

With a sigh he felt down to the depths of his soul, Blaine set Bridgette down on the floor again. But as he did so, he allowed the length of her body to slide provocatively along his. Just so that she would know what she was turning away from. A tempestuous union that promised to be divine.

If a bolt of lightning had just raced up and down her torso, Bridgette couldn't have felt a more electrifying sensation.

Her breathing was ragged and though she was bent on retreating, her hands were still on his shoulders for support.

"You're not being fair."

He smiled. It wasn't an accusation he could deny. "Neither

are you." He feathered his fingertips along her face, caressing her. Her eyes fluttered shut, then sprang open again. "I want you, Bridgette."

How could a man's voice sound so seductive? "You have a son."

Was she really as selfless as she let on? It amazed him. "He's too young for you."

Bridgette tried to rally her flagging defenses and reached for the only weapon she had, anger. But her hold on it was weak. "It's not a joke."

"No," Blaine agreed, growing serious. "Mickey's not a joke." His eyes held hers. "And neither is what I'm feeling. What you're feeling." His expression dared her to deny it.

She shook her head a bit too vehemently. "You haven't the slightest idea—"

He wouldn't accept her protest. He knew better. "Don't I? You want to make love with me as much as I want to make love with you."

She hated the fact that he was right. Hated it because it made such a mess of things.

"Don't get smug." Swinging around, she walked quickly toward the front door. She had to get away from him before she succumbed to him and herself. Before she stayed and begged for more.

She was almost running. He didn't want her leaving like this. Blaine hurried after her and reached Bridgette just at the front door. He caught her by the arm and turned her around to face him.

"See you tomorrow?"

"What?" Not waiting for an answer, Bridgette pulled away. She managed to open the front door and hurry outside. The evening air helped neutralize the feel of his hand on her skin.

He was right behind her, but this time Blaine made no effort to touch her. "The piano lesson. Mickey told me that you come over twice a week. You have another lesson with him tomorrow."

Tomorrow was too soon to go through all this again. She needed time to compose herself, time to think this through. Time to make up excuses that she could believe. "No, I don't think—"

He knew what she was going to say. Instinctively, he knew how to stop her. "Afraid?"

The egotistical jerk. Did he think she was some kind of a shrinking violet he could bowl over with that mouth of his? "I'll be here."

"Good."

No, Bridgette thought as she silently got behind the wheel of her car and slammed the door. Not good. Not good at all.

Gunning the engine so that Blaine was forced to spring away, she pulled out of the driveway. She'd slowed down and was in control by the time she righted the car onto the street, but that didn't help make sense of the turmoil she was feeling.

She wanted to be there for Mickey. Her godson was beginning, just beginning, to come around, like a tiny green shoot of grass that was pushing its way up through the newly warmed soil after a long, cold winter. She couldn't do anything to risk that shoot not coming through. She certainly couldn't just abandon him.

But if she was there, she'd have to face Blaine. And she had no idea how long she could hold out against him. Against what was going on between them.

She was going with someone, she reminded herself for the dozenth time. A nice, stable man. If his polite, passionless kisses didn't reduce her to the consistency of rice pudding, so be it. There were more important things than excitement. More important things than feeling your blood rushing through your veins and echoing in your ears.

For the life of her, Bridgette couldn't think of a single one.

"You are still up, Brita?"

Sophia Rafanelli looked at her granddaughter in surprise as

she walked into the kitchen. Bridgette was sitting at the table, toying with a nearly empty glass of soda. Sophia had seen the light on when she had let herself into the house. Muttering about the fact that Gino always left the lights on, she'd walked in, expecting to find no one. It was not an occurrence that happened often. It gladdened her heart that, for one reason and another, both her son and her granddaughter had temporarily moved back home. Sophia did not take any of it for granted.

The song that she had been humming abruptly faded when she saw Bridgette. Her granddaughter looked more unhappy than she had seen her in a long time.

She cocked her head. Strands of sleek black hair brushed along her shoulders. "You are waiting for me, *bella?*"

Bridgette glanced at her watch. "You should keep more respectable hours, Nonna."

A lusty laugh met Bridgette's comment. "I do. In Italy the day is only beginning." She rolled her expressive eyes as she remembered the evening. It had turned out to be a very romantic one. "Ah, that Jack, he makes me feel like a young girl again. Every dance he insists on dancing." She glanced at her feet. They were beginning to ache, but it was a small price to pay. "If we continue doing this, I will need new shoes very soon."

Her smile faded abruptly, like the sun receding in the face of a rain cloud. Sophia sat down opposite her granddaughter. She slipped off her shoes beneath the table. "But you did not stay up to listen to an old woman carry on."

"Old?" Despite the dilemma she'd been wrestling with, Bridgette felt her mouth curving in a smile. "Nonna, you're younger than I am."

Sophia laughed, delighted at her granddaughter's observation. She prided herself on being the youngest grandmother in her circle of friends, both in age and in looks.

"Up here, little one." She tapped a temple that was completely devoid of gray hair, a feat accomplished by genetics rather than chemicals coming out of a bottle. "That is where you stay young."

That wasn't very encouraging right now. Bridgette looked down at her folded hands on the table. "Then I'm in danger of being a thousand years old."

Sophia placed her hand over Bridgette's. They were supposed to have all gone out together tonight. The last-minute change in plans had surprised her. Perhaps there had been a fight in the aftermath.

"Is it Roger?"

Bridgette nodded. "Yes." But it wasn't Roger, it was her. "No."

Perfectly shaped eyebrows drew together over eyes the color of bright sapphires. "This is difficult for me to take sides in, Brita." Sophia looked at Bridgette, as if to coax a clear answer from her. "Can you, perhaps, be more specific?"

Bridgette shrugged and attempted to begin at the beginning of this tangled mess. "Roger is everything I ever thought I needed in a man."

Sophia heard things she knew Bridgette had no knowledge that she was saying. "Needed, or wanted?"

Bridgette tilted her now-empty glass. A bead of soda trickled from one side to the other, like a chocolate-colored tear. She was vacillating, just like that drop, she thought. "Both, I guess."

Sophia shook her head, discounting Bridgette's words. "They are not the same." She held her granddaughter's gaze. "You may need a shot for measles, but you do not particularly want one."

Bridgette knew what Nonna was telling her. She felt she should somehow be defending her relationship with Roger. It was Blaine who was the interloper here, Blaine who was setting everything on its ear, who had stirred up memories from her own past and was blasting everything apart. "Roger's a good man."

"True." Sophia nodded. She paused for a moment. "So is the mailman."

Bridgette had no idea why Nonna was dragging him into this. "What?"

"Mr. Henderson," Sophia continued, undaunted by the confusion on her granddaughter's face. "He brings the mail to my door if there is a package. That is a very nice thing to do, no?"

Bridgette had no idea what she was talking about. They were discussing Roger, not an elderly mailman who brought packages. "Yes, but—"

"Exactly." Sophia held up one crimson-tipped finger. "'But.' I would not think of marrying him. And neither would you."

The light dawned. "You're twisting things."

It was all a matter of how you looked at something, Sophia thought. She had the benefit of experience on her side. Experience she wanted to pass on to Bridgette.

"No, I am making them a little clearer for you, Brita." It was time to get to the heart of the matter. Sophia leaned closer. "Do you love Roger?" It was something she hadn't asked Bridgette before, but she felt she knew the answer.

That was the million-dollar question. The one Bridgette asked herself as she lay alone in bed at night, staring at the ceiling. "I think so."

Sophia threw her hands up and rose. She had just verified her answer. Now it remained to make Bridgette understand.

"Love is not something you 'think' about. It is something that 'happens.' You *feel* it. Here." Sophia fisted her small hand and beat it twice against her breast. "It soars through your veins like hot, pounding blood." She emphasized each word. "It is *not* like lukewarm tea, left on a table, forgotten." She closed her eyes and let herself embrace the memory. "It is like steaming, strong coffee, opening your senses, making you alert."

"Keeping you up at night."

Sophia's eyes flew open in a look of delight. Bridgette finally understood. "Exactly."

Nonna was describing something that Bridgette felt when

she was around Blaine. It was a caffeine attack, nothing more. Certainly not—

Bridgette looked at her grandmother. "You don't like Roger, do you?"

Sophia spread her hands wide, the portrait of innocence.

"Of course I do. As an accountant, he is wonderful." Some of the enthusiasm faded from her voice. "As a grandson-in-law? Ahh." She stretched out her hand, palm down, and waffled it back and forth to signify her feelings. "Not so much." The next moment she waved a hand at her own testimony. "But what I feel is of no importance." Holding on to the back of Bridgette's chair, she leaned forward so that her face was level with her granddaughter's. "It is how *you* feel that matters here."

Sophia straightened. She'd seen what she wanted to. "And your eyes show me that you do not feel very much. Not for him. Not for Roger." A coy expression slipped over her face. "Is there someone else?"

Coyness wasn't something Nonna could always carry off, not when it came to those who loved her. She didn't succeed now with Bridgette. "You wouldn't be asking that if you didn't already have the answer."

Sophia clapped her hands together, amused at being caught. "I confess, Jack talks." She smiled widely. "Sometimes."

Bridgette could only laugh as she shook her head. Her grandmother was incredible. "Nonna, you're scandalous."

Her smile widened as Sophia accepted her due. "Yes, and I love it." She winked broadly. "It clears the complexion, even at my age." She shrugged. "But we are not talking of Jack and me. We are talking of you and Blaine." She eyed her granddaughter. "Are we not?"

There was no point in denying it. She could never lie to Nonna, even as a little girl. "Yes." She dragged a hand through her hair.

Sophia nodded knowingly. Even if Bridgette had denied it, her actions would have given her away. "And you are confused."

Bridgette sighed deeply. That was the word for it. "Oh, yes."

Sophia saw no reason for confusion, only celebration. "Why?"

Searching for the right words, words that made sense to both of them, Bridgette spread her hands helplessly. "Because, all these years, I've pictured Blaine O'Connor as a monster."

Sophia looked at her knowingly. "And now the monster has a pleasing form?"

Bridgette would have given anything to deny that, to say that it didn't affect her. "Yes."

Sophia had seen the young man for herself. She knew first-hand that Blaine O'Connor looked as if he could set anyone's heart beating fast. But looks alone wouldn't have set Bridgette aflame. Her granddaughter wasn't like that. "And a soul?"

Bridgette looked at her blankly. "What?"

"Soul," Sophia repeated patiently. "You are my granddaughter." She saw bewilderment in Bridgette's eyes and shook her head. "Surely you have not been in his company and not looked into his soul."

Bridgette smiled sadly. If she could do that, then she wouldn't be this confused about things. "It's not exactly like having a crystal ball, Nonna."

Did the girl think she was talking about magical power and witches? Bridgette knew better than that, Sophia thought.

"No, it is having intuition," Sophia insisted. "Something I have passed on to you. Something," she added, remembering, "that sadly skipped your father entirely." Sophia Rafanelli loved her older son, but Carlo had no sensitivity, no empathy. He should never have been blessed with a child. "Gino is different. He is like us, but that is neither here nor there." Like a dove gliding onto a perch, Sophia settled into the chair again and fixed Bridgette with an intense look. "What is this Blaine like?" She wanted to hear the assessment in Bridgette's own words.

Where did she begin? "Well, Diane—"

Nonna stopped her immediately. "No, I am asking you." She pointed at Bridgette. "No one else. What is he like?"

Bridgette bit her lower lip, attempting to discount what Diane had told her. Nonna was right. She had to be fair about this. "He's confused."

Sophia beckoned with both hands, urging the words out faster. "About?"

"How to be a father."

Sophia laughed out loud. That couldn't be what was troubling her granddaughter.

"At times, I am still confused about how to be a good mother, a good grandmother." She smiled at Bridgette. "Even a good woman." She paused, reconsidering, then waved the last part away. "No, maybe not that. But in any case, Blaine's confusion cannot be held against him. What else? Your own thoughts now," Sophia cautioned.

Bridgette shook her head. "But that's just it. My head is all full of what Diane said…" Her voice trailed off as she looked at Nonna significantly.

Sophia peered into Bridgette's eyes and saw the child she had comforted. The child she had held to her breast and let cry when her older son left Bridgette in her care and moved on. "And you remember your father."

Bridgette set her mouth grimly. "Yes."

Her heart was heavy. "I am sorry I could not have given you a better father."

Bridgette looked at her sharply. "It wasn't exactly your fault."

Sophia rose, restless. Somehow, it was always a mother's fault, even when it wasn't.

"Perhaps not, but I am still sorry." She pressed her lips together, wondering not for the first time where she had gone wrong with him. What she could have done differently to have changed him. "He should have had more sympathy for you, more love. When your mother died, I think a great deal of him died with her." It was a reason, but a very poor excuse. "He couldn't open up his heart again."

Bridgette didn't buy that. "He got married again."

"Yes, he did." Sophia crossed to Bridgette and took her hands in hers. "To try to put the pain behind him. Unfortunately, you reminded him of that pain. You look very much the way your mother did." Her mother's heart ached for her older son, even as it condemned his actions. "But each man should be judged on his own, not in the shadow of another." She looked at her granddaughter significantly. "Not in the hearsay of another's words."

Sophia regarded Bridgette in silence for a moment, to see whether she understood. She lightly tapped the young woman's temple. "Judge here." Then very lightly, she ran a finger along Bridgette's breast, outlining her heart. "And here. For the heart sees things the mind cannot understand."

Maybe there was something to Nonna's words. But it didn't quell the unrest she felt. The confusion. And it didn't help settle the quandary.

"He kissed me, Nonna."

This didn't come as a surprise. "I guessed that. You would not be so troubled if he had only shaken your hand." Nonna opened a drawer beneath the tiled counter and rummaged through it. She slanted a look toward Bridgette, knowing that she would be able to tell if her granddaughter was lying to herself. "Did you like it?"

Like was such a paltry word in light of her reaction. "Yes."

Sophia's smile was blooming with the speed of a sunflower. "A lot?"

Bridgette had no idea she was emulating her grandmother's expression. "Yes."

Delighted, abandoning her monetary search, Sophia sat down for the third time in the small space of time. Bridgette had always thought of her as a butterfly, lighting for only a moment. An iron butterfly. "Good. I see no problem then."

Oh, but there was, there was. It only raised problems, not solved them. "I don't understand—"

It was a grandmother's duty to show the coming generations the way. "You tell Roger you are very sorry, but he is not the man for you."

She couldn't do that. She couldn't hurt him that way. "It's not that simple."

Sophia blinked, not comprehending Bridgette's reasoning. "Why?"

"Because." Tongue-tied, Bridgette stumbled, looking for words. "Because—" She gestured around helplessly, her motions an unconscious copy of Sophia's. "Because I can't just let passion rule me." She'd done that once and it had made her shut her eyes to Matthew's shortcomings. It had made her a dupe.

Sophia smiled. Bridgette was young, she would learn. Passion was something precious that did not always enter everyone's life. When it did, it was to be treasured. It made a person eternally young.

"No, my darling, but you cannot be without it, either. A life without passion is a life that will make you old before your time." She rose once more and returned to the drawer. "This Blaine, he works, yes?"

"Yes."

"And he returned to be with his son, yes?" It was a rhetorical question.

"Yes."

That proved her point. The man was decent and, unlike her older son, truly cared about his child.

"That shows stability." Triumphant, Sophia took out an ice-cream scoop that had been embedded in the drawer with various other utensils. "And we have already established his passion." She snapped her fingers. As far as she was concerned, the matter was settled. "As I said, it is simple. You are the one making it complicated, Brita."

Sophia paused suddenly as she heard the front door being opened and closed. "Ah, your uncle is home." She held the scoop aloft. "We will all sit and have ice cream, like we did when you were a little girl."

But she wasn't a little girl anymore. "It won't solve anything."

"No," Sophia agreed cheerfully. "But it will taste good and we will share a moment that will be a nice memory for you when you get old." She smiled, her eyes crinkling. Laugh lines were the only ones she possessed and she wore them like a proud badge. "*Bella,* it will be all right, I promise. Just listen to your heart. In the meantime, Jack tells me that you are helping Mickey deal with the terrible tragedy that has happened."

It was a night for feeling helpless, but at least in Mickey's case, she appeared to have been making a little headway. "I sincerely hope so."

Sophia nodded. "Concentrate on that—the rest will fall into place." She glanced impatiently toward the threshold. "Eh, Gino, bring yourself in here. We want to have ice cream and need your skilled surgeon's hand to scoop it out." Bridgette began to rise, but Sophia placed a hand over hers, stopping her. "Let him do something," she whispered. "Men like to feel useful."

Gino walked in just then. Tall, raven-haired, he looked like a slightly younger, male version of his mother. A very sensuous smile creased his lips. He took the scene in, his two favorite women conspiring.

"Hi, kid." Gino crossed to the table and kissed the top of Bridgette's head. "Ma keeping you up, bending your ear about her escapades?"

Sophia waved him into silence. "Never mind about the Ice Capades, we need your strong arm."

He pretended to make a muscle. "My arm you can have. Elizabeth wanted other parts of me." Amusement danced in his dark blue eyes.

"This," Sophia said to Bridgette as she waved her hand at her son. "This is the type of man you should be avoiding."

Gino bent and kissed his mother's cheek. "I love you, too, Ma."

"According to Diane," Bridgette began, feeling a need to clear it from her mind where it had been prying, "Gino's a piker compared to Blaine."

"Piker," Sophia repeated, bewildered. "What is this piker?"

"Someone who isn't as good-looking as me." Gino laughed. "And don't worry, Ma, when I find the woman I'm looking for, I'm going to be the model husband. I'm a one-woman man— I just haven't found that woman." He grinned and the family resemblance was strikingly obvious. "Until that time, of course, I intend to keep on looking."

And the nurses at the hospital where he was interning gave him a wealth of choices to look through, he thought gratefully.

"Scoop." Sophia handed the scoop to him much the way a queen passed a specter to her firstborn. She stood waiting, her eyes raised to his expectantly.

With a laugh, Gino saluted with the edge of the scoop and turned to open the refrigerator.

Nothing was solved, Bridgette thought as she accepted a bowl filled with rum-and-raisin ice cream, but at least things felt a little better.

For now.

Chapter Seven

Her grandmother's midnight ice-cream raid notwithstanding, the situation wasn't getting any better. Not for her, Bridgette thought as she drove down Mickey's block. She turned the car into the driveway. Nearly four weeks had gone by, and she was still in the same state of upheaval as she had been from the very first moment she had encountered Blaine O'Connor.

With one major difference.

After her talk with Nonna in the kitchen, augmented by a few haphazard words of advice from Gino, Bridgette had made up her mind to concentrate strictly on Mickey. He was what was important here, not any mixed-up feelings she was experiencing.

That, at least was going well. Mickey was beginning to show signs of being himself again. The routine she was helping provide for him appeared to be working. And through her prodding, Blaine's shaky steps into fatherhood were becoming less unsteady. She could comfort herself with that.

The rest of it was still very much a shambles.

Bridgette sighed as she pulled up the hand brake. At least she had been honest with Roger. It hadn't been easy for her, facing him. But anything else wouldn't have been right. She'd talked to Roger the very next day and told him the only thing she could. That there "might" be someone else. Feeble as it sounded, it was the truth. Blaine was neither definitely in her life nor out of it. He shimmered through it like a specter of Christmas Future.

Roger had been surprised and hurt. He had offered to wait it out. To wait for her. She could have cried. With all her heart, she wished she'd loved him. But Nonna had been right. She didn't. To lead him to believe that she ever could was wrong.

She couldn't just let him emotionally hang, hoping she would decide to marry him. It wasn't fair, to either of them. It would weigh her down with a responsibility she didn't want to shoulder and give him false hope. So she had told him that he was too fine a man to keep dangling like some fish on a hook. They had ended it amicably, without emotion.

Her conscience was now clear.

Her mind, though, was not. Her emotions were tangled worse than a string of Christmas lights being taken out of the box after eleven months of hibernation. She had no idea what she should do next.

"The rest will fall into place." Nonna's words played themselves over in her head.

"Oh, Nonna, I hope you're right," Bridgette murmured as she got out of her car.

At least she wouldn't have to cope with Blaine today. He had left on an assignment Wednesday morning and wasn't due back until late Sunday night.

That meant she wouldn't have to face him until early next week. It hadn't been easy, but so far, she had managed to avoid being alone with him. She'd made certain that Jack or Mickey were always in the room with them. It was like perfecting a juggling act and she didn't know how much longer she could keep her own feelings in the air.

Bridgette rang the doorbell. As the first note pealed melodically, Spangles began to bark a response from inside the house.

"Hi, Spangles," she called through the door. "Get someone with hands to open up for me."

The next moment, the door swung open. "Will I do?"

Surprised, Bridgette dropped her portfolio, then mentally cursed herself for her infantile reaction. She stooped down to pick up the case. "What are you doing here?"

Blaine bent down to retrieve her case. They both reached for it at the same moment, their hands getting in each other's way. When she pulled back, he looked up at her and grinned.

"I live here, remember?"

"All too well," she muttered as she rose. Why wasn't he away on his assignment? It was getting so you couldn't count on anything. "I thought you were away on a—" She stopped, fumbling for the word he had previously used.

"Shoot," he supplied.

"My sentiments exactly." Annoyed at being caught so unprepared and so skittish, she walked past him into the house.

Blaine laughed as he closed the door. "I managed to finish up two days earlier than scheduled."

Actually, he had practically moved heaven and earth to complete the shoot in record time. The models had been far from happy. The mood was shared by the agency that represented them. But in his drive to return home quickly, Blaine had gotten an amazing amount of work done. The magazine was certainly happy with him for reducing the number of hours necessary to shoot the layouts.

Blaine thought it best if he didn't elaborate that part of the reason he'd hurried was because of her. Because he wanted to see her again. Because he was getting used to her being a part of his days. That would be crowding her, and he had a feeling that she would react just as he might in a similar situation.

He hated being crowded so he didn't want to crowd her. He just wanted her.

But he had hurried the shoot for another reason, as well, one he could safely admit. "I wanted to get back to Mickey."

Bridgette dropped her portfolio next to the piano and turned to look at him. He looked serious. "You really do care about him, don't you?"

She said it as if it were news. Blaine hooked his thumbs on his belt as he approached her. "I've been saying that all along. Why does that surprise you?"

Despite his verbal testimony, it did surprise her. In a way. In another way, she'd been hoping all along that he was serious.

Bridgette picked up her portfolio and began looking through it for music. It unnerved her to have him staring at her like that, as if all her secrets were visible for his perusal. As if he knew the turmoil she was going through. "It's easy to say something. It's a lot harder to follow up on it."

"So I've noticed." Standing behind her, he toyed with a strand of her hair.

He was entirely too close. But with the piano bench in front of her, there was nowhere for her to move. And he knew it.

His breath tickled the back of her neck. She should have worn her hair down. Bridgette could feel her skin tingle. Turning around, she batted his hand away. "Meaning?"

He let his hand drop to his side. "I said I wanted to make love with you. The follow-through, however, is far more difficult than I anticipated."

Bridgette's eyes narrowed to small blue lights. "Is that what this is about?"

He held up his hands in a T formation, calling for a time-out. "Back up, I think I lost you at the junction."

He knew what she was talking about, she thought, angry. He

just liked to hear it. "At the risk of sounding conceited, are you playing at being the perfect father to impress me?"

"No, I was planning on being the perfect lover to impress you." His grin vanished. "I was going to give being the perfect father, or some semblance thereof, a shot for Mickey's sake, not yours. That has nothing to do with you. You just happen to be someone he likes. I happen to be his father."

She frowned, not knowing what to believe. At a loss, she began looking through her music again, although what she planned to teach Mickey was right on top.

"How's Roger?"

Bridgette raised her head slowly to look at him. She wasn't about to tell Blaine that she had broken up with Roger. She certainly wasn't going to admit that he had caused her such mental unrest that it had forced her to tell Roger to find himself someone else. That would *really* inflate his ego.

"He's fine," she answered coolly. "We're going out tonight."

Though she could have sworn his eyes were mocking her, there was a hint of envy in his voice. "Lucky Roger."

She hated lying. The truth hovered on her lips, but she swallowed it. "So, where's my student?"

He nodded toward the back of the house. "In his room, playing video games." Mickey had been in his room, presumably playing the game Blaine had brought him, for the last hour. "Sometimes I think I'd have better luck communicating with him if I found a way to channel through that unit."

Bridgette was already on her way down the hall. "You'd make a very uninteresting video game," she tossed over her shoulder.

Blaine caught up to her in a few strides. "You might be surprised."

No, she thought, she wouldn't be.

There was no monotonous, grating music floating out of Mickey's room as she approached it. That was odd. Looking in, she saw that the TV set was off. Mickey was on his bed, lying on his side, his legs pulled in toward his stomach.

Alarmed, Bridgette hurried to him. She was vaguely aware that Blaine was right behind her.

"Mickey, sweetheart, what's the matter?"

Mickey moaned as he looked up at her. There was misery in his face. "Bridgette, I don't want to have my lesson today. I don't feel so good."

She touched her lips to his forehead and confirmed what the watery look in his eyes already told her. He wasn't burning up, but he was warm.

"Oh, honey," Bridgette said, stroking the boy's forehead, "you're sick. You need to get out of those clothes and get right into bed."

He made no move to do either. He looked too miserable. "I don't wanna be sick."

Perching on the edge of the bed beside him, she smiled at Mickey. "Nobody does." She glanced toward his shelves. They were crammed with games and books he'd received over the years. A few weary, worn-out stuffed animals stood guard over them. "Tell you what, after you get ready, I'll read to you."

"Like you used to?"

"Just like I used to." She rose from the bed, then hesitated. "Need any help?"

Mickey listlessly moved his head from side to side. His denial only convinced her that he did. Her eyes shifted toward Blaine. He was standing on the other side of the bed, looking simultaneously concerned and very much out of his element.

"Why don't you help him?"

Her voice was soft, but he saw the annoyance in her eyes. It glared at him like a lighthouse beacon. Now what had he done?

He had no chance to ask. Bridgette turned and left the room. Left on his own, Blaine approached the boy. "C'mon, Mick, let's get you into those pj's." He looked around the room, at a loss. "Um—"

"They're in the top drawer," she called to him impatiently.

"That would have been my guess," he called back.

She heard the drawer opening and closing again as she leaned against the wall and waited.

Blaine was out in the hall within five minutes. He looked just a little edgy and in no mood to take anything from her.

"Look, I don't fold the laundry or put it away, Jack does that, so I don't know where Mickey keeps his pajamas." He gestured helplessly. "He's ten years old. He changes on his own."

He still didn't get it, did he? "This isn't about pajamas, this is about you not noticing that he was sick. It doesn't just happen magically in two seconds. Didn't you see that he was listless when he came home from school? Didn't it strike you as odd?"

Blaine shrugged, annoyed at himself for having missed it. Annoyed with her for pointing his shortcoming out. "I thought he was tired." It was a struggle not to raise his voice. "Kids do get tired."

She opened her mouth to retort, then shut it abruptly, chastising herself. She was overreacting again, she thought, seeing her father in Blaine's actions. Her father, who would go out with his friends and leave her alone when she was ill. The last time he did, she'd been afraid and called Nonna, who had come over immediately. She had gone to live with Nonna shortly thereafter.

Blaine was making an effort, she reminded herself. She had to help him, not hinder. "I'm sorry."

He nodded, not completely mollified. "It's okay." Then, because she apologized, he relented. "You're right, I should have realized something was wrong. It's just that I'm not tuned in, yet. And I don't know what to do now." He hated this helpless feeling he had. This almost paralyzing fear of making the wrong move, the wrong decision. "I mean, I never had to deal with a sick kid before. I—"

Bridgette placed a hand on his arm. "It's probably just a cold. Some bug he caught at school. This kind of thing happens all the time."

Blaine looked unconvinced and far from reassured. "He felt awfully warm when I helped him get undressed."

"There's some children's aspirin in the medicine cabinet and—" Bridgette paused. Blaine looked like a lost puppy. Her heart went out to him. "Would you like me to stay for a while?"

Relief flooded through him as he took her hand. "Would you?" He wasn't ashamed of admitting that he was in over his head. "I don't want to mess up any more than I already have."

Bridgette smiled. Without thinking, she gave his hand an encouraging squeeze. "You're learning, O'Connor, you're learning." She turned and walked passed Mickey's room, heading down the hall.

Blaine looked toward Mickey, now tucked in under the covers. As usual, Spangles was stretched out across the foot of the bed. His expression bordered on mournful. "Where are you—?"

Bridgette opened the door to the master bedroom. It looked completely different. The wallpaper was gone, replaced by freshly painted light gray walls. It took her by surprise, but she didn't break stride. "Diane kept a thermometer in her bathroom. First thing we need to do is find out how high his temperature is."

Blaine came up behind her. "And then what?" He'd envisioned her in his bedroom a dozen times but never searching for a thermometer for his son.

"And then—" she turned around holding the slender rod in her fingers "—we'll take it from there."

Bridgette read the thermometer and then shook it down. Feeling that having both of them hovering over him would only agitate his son, Blaine slipped out of the room, leaving Mickey in Bridgette's care.

"You've got a temperature, all right." She gave him two junior-strength tablets and a glass of water.

Mickey swallowed, then handed the glass back to her. He watched her with solemn eyes. "Am I going to die?"

Was that what was running through his mind? The poor kid. "Not from a hundred-degree fever you're not." She made certain her voice remained cheerful.

Mickey seemed almost unaware that his hand rested on Spangles' head. "If I died, would I see Mom?"

She thought her heart was going to break and struggled to keep the tears she felt from her voice. "Yes."

He'd thought as much. "Then it wouldn't be so bad, dying."

She gathered him to her. "No, but it's not going to happen for a long, long time, sweetheart. Your mom would have wanted you to stay down here, with us." She looked down into his face and ran her finger along the short slope of his nose. "We need you." The dog moved on the bed, drawing her attention to him. "What would Spangles do without you?" She smiled as Mickey looked down at the animal. "Who would love him?"

Mickey thought her question over very carefully. "Grandpa?" he guessed.

"Maybe," she pretended to consider his answer. "But not like you can. Little boys' love is very, very special. Dogs know these things." She looked solemnly at the dog. From the corner of her eye, she saw Mickey imitating her. "Spangles knows it, don't you, boy?"

As if taking his cue, the dog barked in reply. Bridgette laughed as she saw a small smile emerge on Mickey's face.

"Okay," he said with a huge sigh. "I guess I won't die."

"That's my guy." Hugging him, she kissed him soundly on the cheek. "Okay, let's see what those pirates are up to, shall we?"

She opened the book Mickey had selected earlier and began to read.

The pirates in question didn't have an opportunity to be up

to very much. Mickey was asleep before she had the chance to read more than half a page. To be on the safe side, Bridgette continued reading for several minutes longer. Mickey never moved.

Satisfied that he would remain asleep for a while, Bridgette closed the book and set it aside on his nightstand, beside the lamp that always remained on.

"Watch him," she instructed Spangles softly. The dog remained immobile, his eyes trained on Mickey.

Bridgette rose and stood for a moment, observing them both, then slowly tiptoed from the room.

She nearly jumped out of her skin when she bumped into Blaine right outside the door. He'd obviously been standing out in the hall the entire time. Stifling a gasp, she glanced toward Mickey to make certain that she hadn't woken him up. He was still asleep. Bridgette looked at Blaine quizzically.

"Taking notes," he told her.

She shook her head as if she'd missed something. "What?"

"If you're wondering what I'm doing out here, I'm taking notes." The gratitude in his smile reached his eyes. "You're pretty good at this."

She didn't really mind when he slipped his arm around her shoulders as they walked out toward the living room. Somehow, it seemed to fit the moment. "I've got a good memory."

He didn't quite follow her reasoning. "What does that have to do with it?"

It was something Nonna had instilled in her. A method that always assured a child of being treated fairly. "I can remember what it was like to be a kid. What everyone did that felt so right to me." Her mouth hardened just a little, though she wasn't conscious of it. "And so wrong."

Blaine moved his arm from her shoulders and looked at her. "Am I being chastised again?"

She shook her head. "No." She wasn't chastising him. She was chastising her father. A contrite smile curved her mouth.

"I'm sorry about earlier. It's just that—never mind." There was no point in rehashing something from the past. And no point telling him more than he needed to know.

"No, what?" he urged.

She shrugged, not wanting to discuss it. But she had jumped down his throat earlier. Maybe she owed him an explanation, to make him understand. "You pressed some buttons earlier."

He knew there were buttons he wanted to press. He just wasn't sure he'd found them, yet. "Good buttons or bad buttons?"

"Both." He arched a brow, waiting. "The bad ones remind me of my father." Uncomfortable with the topic, she felt she'd already said too much. "But you don't want to hear about that."

"Yes, I do." His voice was warm, coaxing. "I want to hear anything you have to say." He smiled, although the memory that suddenly flashed through his mind was not one to smile about. "As long as it doesn't involve throwing dishes at me."

She looked at him oddly. Did he think that just because she had a temper, she'd throw things at him, as well? "I don't throw dishes."

He nodded. "That's comforting to know."

And then she remembered. Diane had been very graphic in describing one of her arguments. She'd thrown dishes at Blaine. One had shattered against a wall right next to Blaine. A flying fragment had caught him just above the eye.

Squinting, she could see a tiny scar there.

Suddenly at a loss, she looked around. She realized that she hadn't seen Jack during all this.

"Where's Jack?"

"He went out earlier, said he was going to play poker with some of his old buddies from the force. He's not supposed to be home until late." That was part of the reason he'd felt so unnerved earlier when he realized that Mickey was ill. "I guess you'd better call Roger."

"Roger?" She looked at Blaine blankly. "Why?"

Had she gotten so wrapped up in taking care of Mickey, she'd forgotten? She was either completely selfless, or Roger didn't mean as much to her as she pretended. "To tell him that you'll be late." He studied her face, curious. "Won't he be worried? I would, if you were late meeting me."

She'd completely forgotten about the lie she'd told Blaine. There was an odd look on his face. She wondered if he suspected the truth.

Bridgette hurried to the living room and picked up her portfolio and her purse. She slung the latter over her shoulder. "I'd better be going…."

She gave him the impression she was running. Not to Roger, but from something. Why? Blaine moved so that he blocked her way to the door.

"Stay." The entreaty seemed to come of its own volition.

The look on his face had her wavering inwardly, but she shook her head. "I don't think that's such a good idea."

"Because of Roger?" He found himself hating a man he didn't know, because Roger had her trust and he didn't. Because Roger could enjoy the feel of her body and he couldn't.

"Because it just wouldn't be a good idea," she repeated stubbornly.

She was beginning to think that Blaine had the makings of a decent father within him, but she wasn't entirely convinced that all of Diane's allegations were entirely groundless. He worked with beautiful women and was continually surrounded by temptation. She didn't want to wake up someday and find herself in Diane's unenviable position of feeling as if she were competing. Besides, Matthew wasn't so far in her past that she wasn't a little gun-shy of falling for a good-looking man.

She wanted to stay, he thought, but she was afraid that he would try something. "How about if I promise to keep my hands at my sides at all times?"

It didn't make a difference. He didn't need his hands to

make her feel as if she were coming unraveled, like a ball of yarn let loose down a hill. All he needed was his mouth. Bridgette shook her head.

It wasn't in his nature to beg, to actively pursue where he wasn't wanted, but he had already broken both rules. He broke a third.

"Bridgette, please. All I want to do is talk." He played his ace card, but it wasn't done for his own gratification. He played it honestly, and meant what he said. "And to have someone here in case Mickey wakes up. In case he needs something. I haven't flown solo, yet. I need a little more confidence. Granted he doesn't have pneumonia or anything like that, thank God, but I'd just feel better if you were here."

How could she turn him down after that? The answer was simple. She couldn't. Bridgette knew that Mickey would be all right, but she could empathize with Blaine's feeling of help-lessness. Empathize with it and give him points for having it.

She wondered if he realized that he had used the most per-suasive argument of all on her. She let her portfolio and purse drop on the sofa. "All right, I'll stay until Jack comes home."

"Thanks. You can use the telephone in the kitchen to call Roger," he prompted.

Roger. She'd forgotten about him again. Bridgette thought about the rhyme about the tangled web being woven once a lie began. She was being deceitful, but pretending that she was still going with Roger was her safety net. It gave her a way to bow out gracefully when she needed it. If Blaine thought she was still with Roger, maybe he wouldn't try anything now that he was indebted to her.

Who was she kidding? she thought as she walked to the tele-phone.

Probably just herself.

She paused before the wall phone, debating turning around and telling Blaine the truth. Her conscience nagged her.

No, this way was better. She'd cut bait as far as Roger was concerned, but she didn't want to get involved with someone who could break her heart. She wasn't the type for casual flings and that, she was sure, was all Blaine was ultimately capable of.

Why limit yourself to having steak every night when there was a smorgasbord waiting for you?

Making up her mind, Bridgette tapped out the numbers on the keypad. She then spent three minutes explaining to the recording at the time station why she wasn't keeping her date tonight.

When she hung up, she turned to find Blaine entering the kitchen.

She moved away from the telephone, as if it would testify to her deceit at any moment. "Afraid I'd make a break for it out the back door?"

"No." He nodded toward the coffeemaker. "I thought I'd offer you some coffee."

She flushed. "I guess you probably think I'm suspicious by nature."

He grinned. "The thought crossed my mind. So, coffee?"

Love was like steaming, strong coffee.

Bridgette blinked, banishing Nonna's words from her head. She wasn't in love with Blaine, she was just attracted. Really, really attracted.

"Yes," she said. "I'd love some." She moved toward the threshold. "I'll go wait in the living room."

She'd just entered when she heard what sounded like something falling. "Everything all right?" she called toward the kitchen.

"Everything's fine," he answered. It sounded as if there was a smile in his voice.

Blaine joined her a few minutes later, sitting down on the sofa beside her. He had a cup in each hand and offered her one. "I guessed that you like cream and sugar."

She looked at him, surprised. "You're right."

"Actually," he confessed, waiting for her to take a sip, "I

didn't guess. Jack told me you liked it that way in passing the other day."

She thought it was rather an odd thing to say "in passing." Was he asking questions about her? Why? And why did that make her feel so vulnerable, as if open season had just been declared on her and she was the only game in the forest?

There was a look in his eyes that she couldn't quite fathom. It bordered on amusement, but she wasn't certain what he was being amused by.

He set his own cup down on the coffee table, untouched. "I'm glad you decided to say. I'm really grateful."

Bridgette held on to her cup with both hands, needing something to do. Needing to keep something in the way just in case he decided to lean over and kiss her. If he did, she could quickly dump the contents in his lap. Or so she told herself.

"Don't mention it." Her hold on the cup tightened. "It's the least I could do."

"No," he countered. "The least would have been to leave me here to cope on my own."

"Maybe," she agreed. "But that wouldn't have been fair."

His eyes held hers. "And you believe in being fair."

"Yes."

"Always?"

Was this about her accusations. "When I can," she replied slowly.

"And honest?"

"Yes." She leaned back. He was studying her. "What are you getting at?"

Was it her imagination, or was that smile on his lips bordering on a smirk? "I have a question for you."

She had a feeling she wasn't going to like what he was about to ask. "All right." Bridgette braced herself. "What?"

"Why did you break your date with the time lady?"

Chapter Eight

Bridgette thought she was choking. The sip of coffee she had taken was stuck in her throat, feeling as if it were taking on width and breadth. Her eyes turned watery.

Blaine quickly took the coffee cup from her hand and thumped her twice on the back. He watched her face carefully.

"Are you all right?"

She waved away the question. Her mind had locked onto his previous one and frozen there. Clearing her throat again, she looked at Blaine warily.

"What did you say?"

He nodded toward the kitchen. "That noise you must have heard a couple of minutes ago?"

"Yes?" She said the word guardedly, failing to see the connection.

"I backed up against the telephone and accidentally knocked the receiver off the hook with my shoulder. When I made a grab for it, I must have brushed against the ReDial button."

The number on the LCD display had struck a vague, familiar

note. Then, as he'd begun to hang up, he heard a singsong voice coming from the receiver.

"That was at 7:23 and six seconds." He grinned as he looked at her. "You called the time station instead of Roger. Unless there's something about Roger you haven't told me—"

She let out a huge breath that would have made the Big Bad Wolf envious. "I lied."

His brows arched as far as they could on his forehead. "No."

Bridgette rose indignantly to her feet. That was it, she was leaving.

At least, she would have left, had she the use of both arms. But one of them was firmly grasped in Blaine's hand. His fingers encircled her wrist like a steel bracelet. Bridgette glared at him, but he wasn't about to release her. Not yet.

"Want to tell me about it?"

Why in heaven's name would she want to do something like that?

"No." She yanked hard and Blaine finally opened his hand.

He nodded, as if accepting her refusal. Partially. "How about if I have Jack ask your grandmother?" he proposed innocently. "He tells me that the two of you are pretty close."

Her eyes narrowed to small slits, like two blue blades intent on slicing him in half. "You leave my grandmother out of this."

"Then tell me." The teasing note was gone from his voice, replaced by sincere curiosity. And something more she couldn't quite fathom. "I know you didn't make Roger up," he said, although that would have been his first guess, "because you and Jack were doubling."

Blaine paused, but she said nothing to fill in the space. He rose to his feet beside her. He was going to have to lead her through this. "Did you lie about tonight?"

Bridgette took the excuse he handed her, thinking it would be the safest way to go. "Yes."

She was agreeing too quickly. Blaine had a feeling that there was more. "Anything else you want to tell me?"

Just why was he so eager to delve into her life? "When you enter the priesthood, then I'll consider making my confession. Until such time, I'll keep my own counsel, thank you very much. Now if you'll excuse me, I have to leave."

He didn't want her to go. More than ever, he didn't want her to go. He placed a gentling hand on her shoulder. "I'm sorry, Bridgette. Stay."

She looked at him skeptically, hating the fact that she was still wavering. By all rights, she should be sitting in her car right now.

"I'll behave," he promised.

"You said that before."

His mouth quirked in a smile that belonged on the face of a mischievous boy. "I'm out of practice—it takes me time to remember how." He looked at her innocently. "I didn't kiss you, did I?"

"No." She hoped that didn't sound as forlorn to him as it did to her.

"And I really wanted to." He smiled into her eyes, into her soul. "That has to put me in line for some kind of a merit badge." He slowly let his hand drift along her arm. She felt the impossibly erotic movement as if she weren't even wearing a long-sleeved sweater. "Besides, the situation hasn't changed any. I still need to have someone here in case Mickey gets worse."

She frowned. The balance on the scale was tipping again. He was making sense. Or did she just want to stay and was searching for a justification?

"All right." She perched on the sofa like a person who expected it to blow up at any moment.

Blaine settled in and made himself comfortable on the opposite end. "Am I allowed to ask you why you lied about tonight?"

She should have known he wouldn't give up on that. "I

thought it would be easier that way." She pinned him with a meaningful look. "Less complicated."

His eyes skimmed along her face. He could almost taste her lips, the way he had a dozen times in his dreams. "I think it's already complicated."

More than you know, she thought, struggling in vain not to react. She searched for a safe topic, mentally summoning Jack home. "So, how did your shoot go?"

There was very little glamour and a great deal of tedious details to his work. "You don't want to know about that."

She looked at Blaine's grin and thought he looked like a cat that had gotten into the cream. "Why? Is there something you want to confess?"

Her words suddenly brought back memories from the past. His grin faded. "Don't spoil this by sounding like Diane." He leaned forward, his eyes holding her in place. "You want to know? Okay, the truth is, it went by so fast, I hardly remember any of it. It was like a thousand other shoots, except faster."

The humorless note in his voice gave her a chill. He sounded like a defendant hardened by countless cross-examinations. Countless accusations, she thought with a twinge of guilt. She'd always seen Diane's side of it. Now she began to wonder about his. It had become evident to her in the last few weeks that Diane had made life very difficult for both of them.

"Why did you marry Diane?"

He looked at Bridgette sharply. Her voice was so soft that for a moment he thought he'd only imagined the question. But it was obvious by her expression that she'd asked it. He had planned to ask *her* questions; he wasn't prepared for the tables being turned.

But perhaps, if he was honest with her, she would be the same with him. He still thought that there was more to this Roger lie he'd caught her in than she was admitting.

"That's simple." At least it had been at the time. "I fell in love with her."

Diane had always bewailed the fact that Blaine had never loved her. "Surrounded the way you were by all those models?"

He would have thought that Bridgette, with her endless font of optimism, would have understood. "Just because you work in an ice-cream factory doesn't mean that you don't want three square meals a day. Ice cream can get pretty old very quickly."

Odd that he'd chosen that metaphor. It made her think of Nonna and her midnight raids. Some of her fondest memories were tied up in those sessions. "I love ice cream."

Any other time, he would have thought she was being contrary. This time was different. Her expression was different, soft, dreamy. "What flavor?"

"All flavors." She stopped to think. If forced to choose, she supposed she could. "Mint chip. I could eat it forever."

It was the first flavor she remembered ever having. Gino had bought her a cone. She had worshipped him at the time the way only a little girl could worship an older relative who seemed nearly perfect.

Blaine let his eyes drift slowly along the length of her torso. That wasn't a body that was constructed out of ice cream. He laughed with a shake of his head. "Better man than I, Gunga Din. I need something with more substance when I'm hungry."

The last word seemed to vibrate between them. Bridgette could almost physically feel the pull between them. The excitement that palpitated just beneath the surface.

She shifted. There was only so far she could go on the sofa before falling on the floor. It wasn't far enough. It still felt as if he were actually touching her. Sensuality seemed to radiate from him. She had to ask. "Was Diane right about you?"

He knew the kinds of things Diane had accused him of. Had she related them all in mushrooming detail to Bridgette? More than likely. It shouldn't have bothered him. But it did. Because Bridgette believed them. Or had. "I never cheated while that ring was on my hand."

She looked down at his hand in surprise. "You wore a ring?"

There were times, even now, that he missed it. Missed what it signified. A dream. One that wouldn't come true.

"It was a double-ring ceremony." He rubbed a thumb over the empty space. "I expected to wear mine for a long, long time." He smiled to himself as he turned the words over in his mind. The smile didn't reach his eyes. "Funny how your expectations wind up changing over the years."

There was something ominous in the way he said that. "Why?" Without realizing it, she drew closer. "What expectations do you have now?"

"None." The word echoed between them. It seemed incongruous with the smile on his face. "That way I don't get disappointed."

It was the first glimpse she had had into his pain. "You don't have anything to look forward to, either."

He lifted a shoulder carelessly and then let it drop. "Those are the breaks." He settled back again; his eyes pinned her. "All right, I answered your question, now you have to answer mine."

Bridgette became instantly defensive. "I didn't know we were trading information."

"We are," he affirmed simply. "How else are you going to trust me?"

She didn't want to get into that, not when she had just lied. "What makes you think I don't trust you?"

His laughter rumbled, low and sensual, as his eyes held hers.

She supposed that it had been pretty evident in her treatment of him. "All right, why *should* I trust you?"

His smile softened, taking on more serious lines. "Because you're the sort of woman who makes up her own mind—eventually," he added when he saw the flush rise to her cheeks. "And I'm a trustworthy sort of person," he concluded. "Besides, we have some things to clear up. I get the definite feeling that there are a whole bunch of people standing between us." He ticked them off on his hand. "Diane, Roger and someone else who didn't treat you very well." He knew by the sudden set of her mouth that he had guessed correctly. "Who?"

Damn, she hadn't bargained on this. "It wasn't a question of mistreatment, exactly."

"But—?"

Bridgette shrugged, not willing to go into it. It hurt enough on its own, without digging it up on purpose.

But Blaine wasn't willing to retreat. Not this time. "You said I pushed some bad buttons. How am I going to know not to push them again if you won't tell me what they are?"

Maybe she had better leave. There was no reason to believe that Mickey wouldn't just sleep through the night. She'd check on him and then go home. "I wouldn't worry about it."

"But I do."

The sincere, sensual note in his voice had her relenting against her own common sense.

"If nothing else, you're Mickey's godmother, as you so haughtily pointed out the first time I met you. You're important to him." Like a lawyer building his case, he went over the particulars carefully, watching her face to see if he was getting through to her, if he was breaking down her defenses. "That means we'll be seeing a lot of each other, one way or another."

Bridgette had the distinct feeling that he was putting her on notice. And that if she wasn't prepared for whatever happened, she had only herself to blame.

His hand slipped over hers. Hers was cold and he wanted to take it between his own to warm it. But he didn't. He didn't want her pulling away from him. "I need to know what I'm doing wrong with you so I don't do it again."

She closed her eyes, summoning strength. It was flagging. "You're not doing anything wrong with me."

This wasn't making sense, but he thought it might if he listened long enough. "Go on."

She shrugged helplessly. "It's just that you remind me of my father."

"Oh, great." Obviously the reminder wasn't a good thing. Was he going to have to fight another set of preconceived notions, after finally—he hoped—having shattered the ones Diane had handed Bridgette?

She shook her head, not wanting him to get the wrong idea. "Not in the way you look or anything, just—"

The last word hung in the air like a link in a chain waiting for the next one to be forged. She took a deep breath, making her decision.

"When I was about Mickey's age, I got sick. I mean really, really sick. I came home from school, feverish and miserable. My father gave me an aspirin and told me to lie down. He had this big night planned with a woman he was seeing." The woman who eventually became her stepmother. Bridgette waved her hand vaguely, forcing back annoying tears at the same time. It always hurt to remember that her father hadn't cared enough about her to be concerned. "And he left. It wasn't the first time he'd done it, but this time really hit me hard."

Blaine had trouble comprehending what she was saying. He was all thumbs at this parenting thing but not from lack of caring. He couldn't conceive of a parent actually behaving in that kind of a manner. "He left you? Just like that?"

She shrugged, wishing she could shrug off the effect the memory had on her. Time had taken some of the sharper edges off, but not the pain. "He figured I'd be okay."

It still didn't make any sense. "Why didn't he call someone to stay with you? A sitter?"

There were excuses for his behavior and at one time or another, she had made them all. None of them bore any weight.

"Money was kind of tight and he thought I was old enough to stay by myself."

"No ten-year-old is old enough to stay by herself." He said it with such feeling, she stared at him in surprise. Something warm stirred within her. "Did your grandmother live anywhere near you then?"

She nodded. But before he could ask why she hadn't been summoned, Bridgette answered, "My father had had a huge fight with her." She set her mouth grimly, remembering. She had never seen her grandmother truly angry before then. "About me, about his neglect. He wasn't about to ask her any favors."

Blaine moved closer, silently offering his support as he slipped his arm around her. "What happened?"

Because he sounded as if he really were interested, she told him.

"I became worse. And frightened. A house is a big, scary place when you're all by yourself at night and sick. He'd ordered me not to, but I called Nonna. I felt like a traitor. Nonna came right over with Gino in tow. She stayed with me all night and gave my father hell when he came home." Bridgette could still hear all the words clearly, even though most of them had been in Italian. "Shortly thereafter, my father left me with her." There were rings forming on the coffee table beneath the cups. She wiped them away with her hand, avoiding his eyes. "At first on weekends, then permanently."

Bridgette sighed, pushing the memory back into the little imaginary box within her heart where she kept it.

"He just wasn't cut out to be a father." She flashed Blaine an apologetic look. "I guess when you were so oblivious to Mickey's being sick, it brought all of that back to me."

He drew her closer to him. There was nothing but comfort in the gesture. "I'm sorry."

She shook her head. "Don't be. I shouldn't have jumped all over you like that."

"No," he clarified. "I mean about your father. It must have been rough on you."

She had every intention of shrugging off his sympathy. She hadn't told him because she wanted his pity. But when she looked into his eyes, her defensiveness melted. She heard herself telling him something she hadn't even admitted to Nonna.

"It still is, at times. I'm lucky to have Nonna and Gino, but you never quite shake off that need for parental approval. At least I can't, not completely. I always wonder what I could have done to have made him like me." She bit her lip. "I guess that sounds kind of dumb."

"No, it doesn't." He'd had parents who cheered him on in basketball games in high school. They had been totally supportive of him whenever he needed them. It was something he'd just taken for granted until this moment. "But did you ever stop to think that it was him and not you?"

"Logically? A thousand times. Emotionally…" Bridgette's voice trailed off.

Emotions weren't things that could be turned off and on, or reasoned with, not really. She slanted a look at him and knew that, eventually, her emotions would be her undoing with Blaine, as well.

"That's why I'm so adamant about your relationship with Mickey. I don't want Mickey to feel the way I did. Anything that might have come before can be negated now, while he's still so young. While his heart is still so open to you."

Blaine understood what she was trying to say. While he didn't feel he'd done anything to match the caliber of what Bridgette's father had done to her, he still needed all the help he could get.

"Thanks. And by the way, thanks for your message."

She'd forgotten all about that. Bridgette sat up and looked at him. "You got it?"

"Yes."

He'd returned to his hotel the first night, exhausted beyond words, and been surprised to find a message from Bridgette waiting for him. At first, he'd been afraid that something had happened to Mickey, but then he'd read further. Bridgette had called to remind him to bring Mickey a gift. Children, she'd made sure the desk clerk added, like getting gifts.

"So?" she prodded. "What is it? What did you get him?"

The only break he'd taken in two hectic days was to go to a toy store. "I bought him a new video game. That's why I was so certain he was playing it in his room." His mouth curved as he remembered the look on Mickey's face when he'd dug into his suitcase and handed him the gift. "I thought his eyes were going to fall out when I gave it to him. Obviously, I made a good choice." There was pride in his voice. The next moment, it was supplanted by awe. "He hugged me. He hasn't done that since before Diane died." Blaine looked down at Bridgette's face. God, but she felt right, nestled against him like that. He knew he shouldn't get used to it. "Ever think of giving father lessons?"

He made her laugh and she appreciated that. "I might pick it up as a new sideline." A thought occurred to her. She'd bet he didn't remember. "Speaking of needing father lessons—"

He resigned himself. "Okay, what did I forget this time?"

She watched his face, knowing that he'd try to bluff his way through this. "Mickey's birthday is coming up."

Blaine groaned.

All right, so he wasn't going to bluff his way through it. There was hope.

"You forgot, didn't you?" Sympathetic tolerance threaded its way through her voice.

He thought of denying it but decided against it. More than likely, she'd only see through him, and so far, the truth was working for him.

"Yeah." He looked at her sheepishly. "I guess with everything that's been going on lately, it just sort of slipped my mind. But I remembered all the other years," he was quick to add. "I don't suppose you know what he'd like?"

She arched her brow, deliberately assuming a cocky stance. "Are you doubting me?"

He shook his head. "Not for a moment."

She had always kept one ear open for things that Mickey let slip, things she'd know he'd like without having to come right out and ask him. "There are souped-up versions of those video games, played on a new unit—"

"Of course."

"But I'm getting ahead of myself." Maybe she'd better write all this down for him.

He liked the way her eyes seemed to shine when she was making plans. They darkened whenever he kissed her. He wasn't sure which color he liked best.

"You? Never."

She gave a playful shove. "Shut up and listen, O'Connor."

He shook his head. "Only if you call me Blaine."

Bridgette rolled her eyes. "Blaine."

"Ohh." He began to nibble on her ear. "Did you know you sound incredibly sexy when you say my name?"

She had to concentrate on remaining still. He was sending an army of shivers through her. "Your name will be mud if you don't listen."

He worked his way along her throat. "Even that sounds sexy."

Planting her hands on his chest, she pushed him away. She couldn't think if he was distracting her like this. "Are you up to a slumber party?"

"Definitely." His smile was pure sin as he looked at her. "Your place or mine?"

She didn't know whether to laugh, hit him or succumb. The latter was quickly becoming the odds-on favorite. "Your place. With about eight little boys."

He shook his head sadly. "You're shattering a fantasy here."

She batted away his hands from her waist. "Get serious, Blaine."

Like twin homing pigeons, his hands returned to her waist. "What makes you think I'm not?"

Bridgette tried to ignore the way his fingers felt on her skin. She was doomed to failure from the very start. "You're making it very hard to concentrate."

"Good." He framed her face.

Definitely doomed, she thought.

"Let's get this out of the way, and then you can talk all you want," Blaine said.

As if I'm going to have any breath left, she thought as his mouth covered hers.

Perhaps it was because she had given up the safety of having Roger to turn to. Perhaps it was because she'd told Blaine about her father. Or perhaps it was because, with his kindness, his humor, Blaine had managed to undermine a little further the image of him that Diane had created for her. But, for whatever reason, Bridgette felt particularly exposed, particularly vulnerable when Blaine kissed her this time.

The only thing that kept her anchored was the thought that there was a sick little boy in the next room, a little boy who might wake up at any moment and need them. If it weren't for that one sobering fact, Bridgette would have been afraid of where this would have led.

Where she desperately wanted it to lead.

Each time his lips touched hers, she had that much less resistance at her disposal, that much more of a need to have him kiss her again. Blaine's kisses weren't pleasant, soothing, mind-settling the way Roger's had been. This was a whole new land she found herself in.

Dark, exciting. Dangerous.

She was risking things, risking giving up herself with absolutely no way of knowing if there would be anything returned in exchange. It was almost certain that there wouldn't be.

Bridgette drew her breath in quickly, to match the tempo of her heart. His hands had left her face. She felt them at her waist once more, working their way up slowly along the sides of her body, sliding to her breasts and curving around the soft swells.

She felt her blood rushing through her, like a volcano threatening to explode. She arched into his touch, her breath ragged as she felt him caress her.

"This is all I thought about while I was away," he whispered against her throat. "All I wanted." Wanting her had verged on driving him crazy. Every time he'd looked through the lens, he'd seen her, in every pose, against every backdrop.

With all her heart Bridgette wished she could believe him. There was still part of her that had to be convinced, had to be won over. But for now, with desire marching through her like a storm trooper, she could pretend that what he said was true.

The sound of the front door being unlocked had them springing apart like two guilty teenagers discovered in the back seat of a car by a patrolling policeman.

Jack, his key still in his hand, looked from one to the other on the sofa. They looked guilty as sin and just a little disheveled. Good, he thought. Blaine made a hell of a better match for her than that Milquetoast Roger.

Jack made no effort to hide the wide smile that sprung to his lips. "I can go out again—" he volunteered, jerking a thumb toward the door.

"No, I was just leaving." Bridgette rose up on very shaky legs and smoothed out her skirt. To her horror, her sweater was askew. She fixed it with as much dignity as she could muster.

"Funny, it didn't look like you were leaving to me." Jack chuckled. He held his hands up before him, palms to the ceiling. 'But then, maybe my vision's getting a little blurry, what with my age and all." He took an accommodating step toward the hall. "I'll just go to my room." He stopped in the doorway. "Did I mention that my hearing is going, too? I might even need a hearing aid."

"Cut it out, Jack," Blaine warned. He looked toward Bridgette, afraid that Jack's teasing was embarrassing her. He didn't want to jeopardize this new step they'd taken. "I'd offer to take you home," he told her. "But then you'd have to drive me back."

"Thanks, I'll pass." She looked at Jack, her momentary fluster abating. "I thought you had a poker game."

Jack shrugged philosophically. "I had the game but not the luck. I never let myself lose more than I can comfortably do without, and my grandson's birthday is coming up. If I'm going to throw money away, it's going to be in his direction."

Bridgette gave Blaine a smug look that seemed to say, *See, Jack remembered.*

Jack's brow puckered in confusion as he noted the exchange. "What? Did I say something wrong?"

"No," Blaine conceded graciously. "I just forgot about Mickey's birthday and Bridgette is silently rubbing it in."

"Sorry," Jack murmured.

"Don't apologize." Blaine laughed. "It beat hearing her rub it in."

"Don't make me hit you again," Bridgette warned.

Blaine leaned toward Jack. "I love it when she gets physical."

Jack liked what he was seeing. "My offer still holds," he volunteered. "I'll even put a pillow over my head."

"No," Bridgette said a bit louder than necessary. "No pillow over anyone's head. We need to make plans for Mickey's party."

Blaine shoved his hands into his pockets. "You still want to have a slumber party?"

Jack rolled the idea over. "Sounds good to me. What does Mickey think of it?"

"He'll love it," Bridgette assured him. It was just what Mickey needed. It was time he mingled with other children again.

Blaine thought of having eight little boys all under one roof and a swarm of qualms set in.

Chapter Nine

Blaine no longer feared hell. He figured that it couldn't be that much worse than being in the middle of an eleven-year-old's birthday party.

At thirty-three, he would have thought that he was equal to the situation; after all, they were only little boys. It didn't work that way, though. Age here was not a helpful factor. The only way it might have been, he decided, was if he had been a thirty-three-year-old lion tamer. Maybe then he wouldn't have felt so outnumbered.

To make matters worse, his ranks had shrunk to one. Him.

As of late yesterday afternoon, Jack had succumbed to the same bug that had previously afflicted Mickey. He'd taken to his bed and remained there today after tendering a heartfelt apology. Sadly lacking in energy, Jack had no strength to face the oncoming horde.

God only knew where Bridgette was.

Blaine winced as he heard an ominous *thud* from the other room. Something else had been broken or maimed. The party had been going for thirty minutes. He felt as if he were lost in no man's land without a map.

Bridgette should have been here by now, he thought, although, if he'd had his choice, he wouldn't have been "here," either. But this had all been her diabolical idea and she should be here to suffer the consequences, instead of leaving him to face it alone.

She'd brought over the cake earlier, while Mickey was still in school, and promised to return by the time the party was under way.

Just what the hell was her definition of "under way"?

There'd been no answer when he'd called her house after the first two boys had been dropped off on his doorstep. Blaine had an image of Bridgette sitting in her living room, a Mona Lisa smile on her face while his voice emanated from her answering machine. He could only hope that the message he'd left was coherent, unmarred by the mounting discomfort, not to mention the panic, that he was beginning to experience.

They seemed to be everywhere. Just how could eight kids move so fast?

On paper, when Bridgette had planned this party with Jack and him last week, it had seemed doable. Eight kids, one video game unit with two added control pads—that had been her idea—and one television set playing the latest action movie for those who were waiting their turn at the video game. It seemed right.

There were also a number of board games set up here and in the family room. In Blaine's estimation, there was something for everyone no matter what they wanted to do.

What everyone wanted, it seemed, except for Mickey, was bedlam.

The noise was getting out of hand. Spangles was adding to the chaos by sporadically barking at one boy or another.

At the moment, the dog was barking at the two boys who were pretending that Spangles was an evil ninja intruder. From what Blaine could make out, they were out to defend the universe from him.

Blaine grabbed one child in the middle of a dramatic swing. "Hey, no karate chops to the dog," he chastised. He bodily deposited the boy on the other side of his friend, who, for the moment, was the more tranquil of the two.

They looked interchangeable, he thought. Did all kids besides Mickey look alike? This parenting was no piece of cake no matter how you sliced it.

The offended would-be samurai lifted an indignant face up to Blaine. "That wasn't karate, that was—"

Blaine had no intentions of getting embroiled in semantics. "Whatever it was, don't do it."

The boys exchanged superior looks, shrugged and rushed off in the direction of Mickey's room. Or so Blaine hoped. He looked around the living room, waiting for the next accident to happen.

"Fine help you are," he muttered to Spangles. The dog only barked in reply and trotted off, presumably to find Mickey.

Blaine had just scooted one eager climber from the arm of the sofa, where he'd been set to dive-bomb in emulation of the action hero on the screen, when he thought he heard the doorbell. Placing the boy on the floor with a warning he knew would go unheeded, Blaine offered up a silent prayer as he crossed to the door.

Please let it be her.

He threw the door open. *Yes, Virginia, there is a Santa Claus.*

"Where the hell have you been?" he demanded heatedly. It only vaguely registered that there was an unfamiliar van parked in his driveway. Had someone given her a ride here?

The coup she'd just managed to pull off made Bridgette far too pleased with herself to allow Blaine's tone to annoy her.

"Stuck in traffic." She moved past him into the living room and then stopped. "Oh, my."

"'My' doesn't quite cover it." Blaine dragged a hand through his hair, wondering where he could get a good cleaning crew and how he'd allowed himself to be talked into this in the first place. "I'm not even sure my insurance quite covers it."

Bridgette quickly surveyed the devastated area. His living room looked like the scene of a recent hit-and-run guerrilla attack. Cushions were drunkenly strewn about. Half-filled soda cans were scattered on almost every surface in the room, and, from the looks of it, two kinds of chips appeared to be permanently ground into the weave of the rug.

"Oh, it's not so bad." Nothing a good cleaning couldn't take care of.

"Not so bad?" he echoed incredulously, gesturing about. Wasn't she looking? "I keep telling them to calm down, but they don't listen."

She should have gotten here earlier, she thought. But talking Alice into postponing her vacation for one more day and bringing her act here had taken time.

Bridgette patted Blaine's arm comfortingly. "They probably suspect that you're a pushover."

The boys had mysteriously retreated into the family room, or parts thereof, he thought, following Bridgette into the next room. The thought of joining Jack and pulling the covers over his head was beginning to sound infinitely appealing.

"I'm not a pushover," he protested. "I'm just not used to dealing with people four feet and under."

That was for sure, she mused. Not en masse at any rate. But he was making headway with Mickey.

She walked into the family room. It was just as bad as the room they'd left. Game board pieces crunched under her shoes. Bridgette gingerly stepped aside.

"Take heart," she told him cheerfully, "the cavalry has arrived."

He had no idea what she could do that he couldn't. Not at this stage. Ropes and tranquilizing darts were probably needed a this stage. "I don't think the natives are about to surrender."

"We'll see."

The woman was too smug for her own damn good, he thought. He would have loved to see her fail if it didn't mean sacrificing his house. Any way he figured it, he was stuck with these kids for another fourteen hours at the very least.

Bridgette stepped in between two boys who were wrestling. Rather than taking each by an arm the way he would have, she merely shook her head.

"Time out!" she called in a voice that was far more forceful than he'd ever heard her use.

Blaine leaned against the wall and tucked his hands in his pockets. This, he thought, might be rather interesting at that.

To his amazement, the two boys ceased wrestling almost immediately. The stockier boy dropped the other one. The latter bounced onto the comfortable padding of his rear before springing to his feet beside his opponent. There was respect in their eyes when they looked at her, Blaine thought in admiration.

Maybe the woman was a witch.

"Where's Mickey?" Bridgette asked the taller of the two.

He shrugged in reply, but the boy Blaine had plucked off the arm of the sofa pointed to the back of the house. "He's in his room showing Darian how to play Snake Men."

That was a good sign. Maybe Mickey was finally taking an active part in things. That was why she'd insisted on this party for him in the first place.

"Thank you." She sounded as if she were addressing the chairman of the board of some corporation instead of a ten-year-old boy with freckles, Blaine thought, amused. "Follow me, men," she said.

And they did. All of them.

Not to be eased out by the crowd, Blaine fell into step directly behind her. He had, in his estimation, the best view.

"How did you do that when I couldn't?" he whispered as they entered Mickey's room.

"Easy." She grinned, patting his arm. "They sense fear. Besides, I'm a teacher, remember?" They'd never made teachers like her when he was a little boy, Blaine thought. If they had, he might have gone on to get a college degree, instead of getting out as soon as he could. "Do you know what a room full of kids with musical instruments sounds like if you don't have a way of projecting authority?"

Blaine could well imagine. He shook his head, as if to keep the thought at bay. "Spare me."

He got the picture, she thought. "Exactly." She had learned very quickly that she could still be their friend and yet maintain that slight distance between them that made her the teacher and them the students.

Bridgette looked into Mickey's room. Mickey was holding one set of the extended control pads she'd brought over yesterday. Pressing buttons, he was using it to explain the fine points of eluding King Asp.

It felt great seeing him like that, playing like a regular little boy, Blaine thought.

Mickey looked up and saw Bridgette. Blaine watched as pleasure spread like rays of morning sunshine on his son's face. The credit for the transformation was all hers. She'd worked magic in his son's life. Step by step, bit by tenacious bit, Bridgette had made that sad-eyed little boy recede.

"Hi," Mickey called out to her.

"Hi, yourself. Happy Birthday, Mickey." She refrained from hugging him, although she wanted to a great deal. Eleven-year-old boys had their masculinity to protect, especially in front of their friends.

"Thanks." He flushed. She was empty-handed, he noticed. "Did you buy me a present?"

Normal, he was getting to be normal. "Sure did. It's in the car. But that's for later. Part of your present is setting up in the backyard right now."

This was the first Blaine had heard about it. "What part of his present?" he asked suspiciously.

Why hadn't she told him she had something else planned? The answer came on the heels of the silent question. Because she probably thought he wouldn't like it.

Which meant he wouldn't.

Bridgette was already walking out of Mickey's room. Like the Pied Piper of Hamelin leading a squadron of mesmerized mice, Bridgette took the boys to the backyard.

She chose not to answer his question immediately. "I had a last-minute brainstorm." Smiling, Bridgette rested one arm along Mickey's shoulder. That much in his budding male world was still allowed, she mused.

Now Blaine *knew* he wasn't going to like whatever it was she had planned. "Should I be running for shelter?"

She looked at him innocently. "Only if you're afraid of snakes, lizards and spiders."

She'd completely lost her mind, he thought. But she did manage, Blaine noticed, to effectively capture the attention of every little boy trailing after her. "You've got snakes?"

There'd been a time when she was younger when she had considered having a pet snake. The horror with which her grandmother had greeted the suggestion had quickly terminated that desire.

"Not personally, but I did bring someone to the party," she said to Mickey rather than to Blaine, "who brought a whole vanload of her friends, and *they're* snakes, as well as lizards, spiders, one very large turtle and a few interesting frogs."

Her announcement was met with a chorus of noise that testified to the fact that frogs, insects and assorted reptiles were of tantamount interest to her entourage.

Not only was he going to have hot and cold running children roaming through his house, but insects and snakes as well? Her announcement left him cold.

Taking her other arm and drawing Bridgette aside, Blaine signaled a halt to the convoy.

"One minute, kids." He lowered his voice as he looked at Bridgette. "You're serious?"

"Perfectly." She smiled at the boys impatiently clustered around Mickey before continuing. "I thought they might be entertained for a while by a little show. From the looks of your living room, I obviously thought right. I let Alice in through your side gate. I hope you don't mind."

It was a little late for that. "Mind? Why should I mind someone bringing a cobra into my backyard?"

"Python," Bridgette corrected, a grin playing on her lips.

Despite the chaotic situation, he would have liked to wipe that smile from her lips in his own fashion. Later, he promised himself. Later.

"Makes all the difference in the world," he quipped sarcastically. "Is Alice the snake or the handler?"

"Handler." She beckoned and the boys followed her into the kitchen.

A woman with an entourage of reptiles, insects and who knew what else? "Where do you *meet* these people?" he marveled.

"I get around." She stopped in the kitchen, waiting for stragglers to catch up.

She looked right in her element; he, however, was not. "So, what made you think of having snakes catered?"

She held the sliding glass door in place, unwilling to let the boys out until she secured their full cooperation. "With kids, you have to improvise." The idea had come to her right after she'd dropped off the cake this morning.

He looked around at the eager faces and began to wonder if any of this was such a good idea. But then he saw the same expression mirrored on Mickey's face and knew that it was.

"Right."

Directly behind her, in the yard, a powerful-looking woman

with what looked like a snake tattooed on her forearm was setting up a makeshift stage area. She was surrounded with boxes that promised to provide a very interesting show.

The boys looked as if they were ready to explode into the yard, but Bridgette held up her free hand, calling for silence.

"Okay, guys, I want you to follow me and sit down on the grass in a semicircle in front of the stage the Lizard Wizard has set up. When you're all ready, she can start the show." She opened the door. "Mickey, you lead."

To Blaine's surprise, the boys filed out behind Mickey like a line of ducks in formation. "Lizard Wizard?"

"Kind of catchy, don't you think?" It was painted in purple across the gray van.

He would have had another word for it. "If you say so."

The boys all sat down quickly, eager to have the show begin. The deafening din he'd put up with just a few minutes ago was a thing of the past. The woman *was* a witch, Blaine thought as he walked behind her into the yard. A very sexy witch.

Alice dispelled her no-nonsense impression as soon as she smiled. "I'm almost ready, Bridgette," she called.

"Take your time, we have all evening." Bridgette sat down behind Mickey.

Blaine squatted down beside her. "Friend of yours?" he whispered.

She nodded. "Yes. Actually, she's the mother of one of my students. That's how I managed to get her on such short notice. I pleaded emergency."

He eyed the long cage that was closest to the house. A very large snake was lying within. It seemed to fill up the entire space. That would be the python.

"Let's hope we don't have one," he murmured to her under his breath.

Alice was about to start. "Shh," Bridgette warned him. "Listen."

Blaine raised an amused brow. "They talk?"

"No, but Alice does. This is very educational." She whispered the last word into his ear, knowing full well how boys that age reacted to anything that was supposed to be informative.

Her breath floated along his skin and he had to remind himself that they were here because of Mickey and a collection of snakes. Reality had a way of shimmering to the back burner whenever he was around her. She even made him forget, for large portions of time, that he didn't believe in marriage as an institution anymore. He'd said as much to her more than once, but now strong doubts were beginning to surface. The right person made all the difference in the world.

For now he had to content himself with being Mickey's father and not someone interested in being Bridgette's lover. Blaine folded his arms before his chest and sat back, ready to be "educated."

She'd been right again, Blaine mused as the hour wore on. The boys who had seemed bent on destroying his house in record time were mesmerized, held spellbound by an affable woman and her unusual collection. A collection she more than cheerfully shared with them.

There'd been only one interruption and that had been in the beginning. Spangles had wanted to single-handedly take on all the reptiles, issuing a challenge to them via a continuous bark. Blaine had to escort the four-legged heckler into the house and close the sliding glass door behind him.

It was a hands-on program, Blaine discovered. Each snake, each lizard and spider in the collection, was taken out of its cage or container and put on display. Alice encouraged the boys to come up, one by one, and handle the creatures. Some she even passed around. She showed them how to hold them.

The boys watched and absorbed, eager to get their turn. Mickey, after some hesitation, agreed to have the garden snake twist around his wrist like a living bracelet. The boys held their breaths as the tarantula walked along someone else's head and down his arm.

The python was the show's finale. "He's a big son of a gun," Alice told the boys. "As I'm sure you can all see. And if you want him out of his cage—"

"Yes!" The cry was unanimous.

"Then I'm going to need each and every one of you to help me."

"As if she could stop them," Bridgette said, laughing, to Blaine.

The boys had all jumped to their feet as if they were joined at the hip as soon as Alice had announced her need for volunteers.

"Wait, there's snake enough for all of you." Alice glanced at Bridgette and Blaine. "You, too."

Blaine was a little uncertain about the matter as he rose, giving Bridgette his hand.

She wrapped her fingers around it and gained her feet. Dusting off her hands, she stepped up to Alice. "Okay, what part do I hold?"

"Right here'll do fine." Alice pointed to a section beside Mickey's. She turned clear, water blue eyes on Blaine. "How about you, Dad? We need something to bring up the rear." She nodded at the end she was holding. "Or would you rather make eye contact?"

The boys giggled. Including, Bridgette noted with no small measure of satisfaction, Mickey.

"The rear'll do just fine, thanks," Blaine answered, mugging for the benefit of the boys.

"Hey Dad, doesn't his skin feel silky?" Mickey stroked his section in awe. "It's not scaly or clammy or anything." The snake wiggled and Mickey nearly dropped his portion. At the last moment he managed to regain his hold.

It was the most enthusiasm Mickey had displayed over anything in the six weeks since he had come to live here, Blaine thought. There was no way to express what he was feeling at the moment. But when he looked at Bridgette, Blaine had the feeling that somehow she knew.

Alice elaborated on Mickey's comment.

"Snakes," she told the little boys solemnly, "have always gotten a bum rap." She grinned as the snake was attempting to wrap itself around her arm. "You should only pardon the expression. Okay, boys, help me get Hilda back into her home."

She coached the boys into returning the python to its cage. All the other snakes had already been put away.

Pleased, Alice looked around at the semicircle of faces. "So, now you all know that snakes are really fine, noble creatures that are a help to the farmer. And, they make interesting pets." She closed the lid on Hilda's cage and secured it.

Mickey looked up at Blaine. "Can I have a snake as a pet, Dad?"

It was the first thing that Mickey had actually asked him for and Blaine found himself at a loss for a reply. He didn't really want a snake slithering around somewhere in the house, but it wouldn't do to say that in front of the boys, not to mention Alice.

He hated refusing Mickey.

"I don't think Spangles would like sharing you, Mickey," Bridgette pointed out. "He didn't seem very happy about the visitors. And you want to be fair to Spangles, don't you? You've had him longer."

Mickey nodded. It made sense. He'd only been caught up in the moment, anyway. "Oh, yeah, okay."

Just like that, Blaine thought, looking at Bridgette. He could have kissed her.

The boys continued to talk about the reptiles and the show itself long after Alice, with the help of eight sets of eager hands, had put the entire collection into her van. It was obvious that the Lizard Wizard had been the hit of the party.

To Blaine, the hit of the party wasn't a woman with reptiles and a tattoo, but Bridgette. The hit and the savior. As far as he was concerned, she had saved his sanity and his house.

With the commanding presence of a general marshalling his troops, she had taken over. Dinner was served within thirty minutes of the Lizard Wizard's departure. Blaine had ordered three large pizzas with everything, as well as one with just cheese.

The boys ate as if they'd been starved for the last three weeks. Coming into the kitchen, Blaine deposited the dirty plates on the counter. He eyed the empty boxes dubiously.

"Think they'll have room for the cake?"

She gave him eight plates and a handful of forks. "How long has it been since you were a little boy?" she asked with a laugh.

Because they were in the kitchen and, for a fleeting moment, alone, he took the opportunity to nuzzle her. "A long time, thankfully."

"Get them ready. I'll bring in the cake."

He sighed. "You have the easy part."

"It's a large cake."

Blaine smiled to himself. Mickey wasn't the only one she was having an effect on.

Bridgette checked her pockets for matches and candles before leaning into the refrigerator. Holding the sides of the platter, she carefully took out the cake she'd delivered earlier.

"Sure you don't need any help?" Blaine came up behind her.

She glanced at him over her shoulder. "You're just looking for an excuse to get fresh."

"Yeah, there's that, too." He grinned. "What are my chances?"

"Get back in there." She motioned toward the dining room with her head.

He grazed her mouth with a quick kiss before crossing to the doorway. "Spoilsport."

"That's me," she quipped as she closed the refrigerator with her back.

Blaine distributed the plates and forks. He'd set down the last plate when she entered carrying the cake. He hadn't had a chance to look at it earlier. Looking over her shoulder, he saw that it was a half-sheet cake. Drawn on top, in vivid colors, was a little boy sitting in front of a television set, playing a video game. The icing drawing bore a striking resemblance to Mickey.

Blaine was amazed at the likeness. "Where did you get that?"

Cake decorating was a hobby she enjoyed. One that she hardly ever got the opportunity to indulge in. "I made it." She placed it on the table in front of Mickey.

Blaine could only shake his head. "You're a woman of rare talents."

Bridgette laughed as she took the box of candles out of her pocket. "You don't know the half of it." She began placing the candles into the cake, making certain that they were close enough for Mickey to blow them all out at once.

No, Blaine agreed silently. He didn't know the half of it. But he meant to. He sincerely meant to.

She handed the matches to Blaine. This was something, he thought, that he'd been deprived of all the other years. Diane had never let him attend Mickey's parties, never let him see the boy on his birthday. He'd had to make do with the day before or after if he was in town. He'd never let Mickey know that it was because of Diane, but he had never forgiven her for it.

As he struck the match, he watched the flame flicker in his son's eyes and felt very blessed.

Blaine blew out the match and stood back.

"Okay, boys, let's hear it," Bridgette coaxed.

A joyful dissonance rose, bearing a distant resemblance to "Happy Birthday." Spangles joined in, barking loudly. When the sounds died away, Bridgette stepped forward and lowered her face to Mickey's.

"Okay, make a wish and blow out all the candles, Mickey."

Mickey paused for a moment. Thinking, he screwed his eyes shut tightly and made his wish. Satisfied that he had done all he could, Mickey blew out his candles. One lone light flickered for a moment, as if undecided whether or not to go out, then was extinguished with the rest.

The boy sitting on Mickey's right cheered. "That means you'll get your wish." He winked broadly. "If it's not very expensive."

Mickey shook his head, his expression serious. "It's not expensive at all."

"What is it?" another boy prodded. It was obvious that the boy didn't think a wish was worth making if it didn't involve something expensive.

Mickey opened his mouth to answer, but Bridgette was quick to stop him.

"No, don't tell." She looked into his eyes, coaxing a smile from him. She'd certainly gotten her wish, she thought when she saw it. "Then it won't come true."

An odd, mysterious smile curved his lips as Mickey nodded. Bridgette had never lied to him and he knew that if she said it, it had to be so. His wish was coming true.

"Okay." Bridgette handed Mickey the knife. "You make the first cut."

Holding the knife just so, Mickey made a long cut in the cake. He frowned at the slightly crooked line.

"Want to cut the pieces?" she asked.

He debated, then relinquished the honors. "Naw, I just want to eat it."

Bridgette laughed as she took the knife from him. She glanced quizzically at Blaine, silently offering the utensil to him. She didn't want him to think she was usurping him.

Blaine waved her on. "You're doing fine without me."

"You're just lazy," she countered.

"Yeah, you might say that," he agreed good-naturedly. This felt right, he thought, watching her like that. Even the party felt right. Maybe he was wrong, worrying about déjà vu. Maybe, just maybe, things could work out if he pushed a little.

Very capably, Bridgette cut twelve equal pieces out of the cake, then laid the knife aside. "Why don't you hand them all out while I take a piece up to Jack?"

He'd completely forgotten about Jack. "You think of everything, don't you?"

She looked at Blaine. No, not everything, she contradicted silently. She hadn't thought of the danger of losing her heart. And she was afraid that was exactly what was happening.

"Most of the time." She looked at Mickey. "Wait until I get back before you open your presents." It was a request.

Mickey nodded, cake outlining his lips. They were curved in a smile.

Nothing short of a miracle worker, Blaine thought. He stared at her retreating form for a moment before getting back to the task at hand. He didn't want the natives getting restless again.

Chapter Ten

In Blaine's estimation, there had probably been more logistics involved in setting up the eight sleeping bags and getting their various occupants into them in Mickey's room than there had been in synchronizing the Allied invasion on D day. But finally, it was accomplished. He'd made certain that each boy had changed, brushed and was settled in. A litter of month-old puppies would have been easier to handle.

When he'd left the room, they were telling creepy stories. With the lights on, in deference to Mickey.

Blaine had faced the chore all alone. Bridgette had insisted on it. He hadn't been very happy about it. Now that it was over, he had to admit that it felt pretty good. Like a toothache that had finally stopped throbbing.

If only *he* could, he thought wearily, glancing at Bridgette as he walked into the living room.

"You know, if we found a way to harness all that energy in there," he said, nodding in the general direction of Mickey's room, "we could probably provide enough electricity to light up Las Vegas until the turn of the century."

She grinned as she threw another empty soda can into the plastic garbage bag beside her. There was another bag next to the coffee table, almost completely filled with ripped wrapping paper.

"Or San Francisco at the very least." Bridgette looked up as Blaine dropped, exhausted, onto the sofa, and she smiled fondly at him. "Welcome to fatherhood."

"Yeah." The single word emerged, riding on a sigh like a surfer taking a huge wave.

Beneath the frustration and the exhaustion was a very definite sense of well-being. It was a good feeling. The one, he knew, that had escaped him all these years. The one that came from enduring the bad times to make the good that much more precious.

"Yeah," Blaine repeated as a grin slowly curved his mouth.

It took him a moment to realize that he wasn't sitting on anything but sofa. There were no game pieces beneath him digging into his flesh, only a cushion. Being wrapped up in his exhaustion had prevented him from focusing on anything else, save his ordeal and Bridgette.

Letting his head fall back, Blaine slowly scanned the room. It bore a strong resemblance to the living room he'd had several hours ago, before the army of munchkins in the back bedroom had descended on it.

While he'd been in there, struggling to bed the troops down for the night, she had been out here, cleaning up. Guilt pricked his conscience, but not too strongly. After all, if she hadn't done this, he would have had to. Eventually.

But form demanded that he go through the motions. "Hey, you don't have to do that."

She deposited the last of the popcorn that had fallen on the floor into the black plastic bag. "Nervous energy." She shrugged without looking at him. "I might as well put it to good use."

He studied her for a moment. Bridgette avoided his eyes only when she was attempting to deny her reaction to him.

"What are you nervous about?"

"Lots of things." She secured the top of the bag with the cans in it. "I'm taking my master's exam in a few weeks." Like a bee buzzing from flower to flower, unable to decide where to settle, Bridgette moved toward the easy chair. She picked up the cushion from the coffee table and set it back on the seat.

She was still avoiding his eyes, Blaine noted, pleased. Some of his exhaustion began to slip away. "You don't strike me as the type to worry about that sort of thing ahead of time." He rose and crossed to her. "C'mon, what is it?"

Bridgette kept her back to him. "Don't fish, O'Connor."

That cinched it. But he still wanted to hear her say it. "It's me, isn't it?"

She glanced at him over her shoulder. "If your grin was any larger, it would split your face."

He slipped his hand around her waist. He figured he'd earned it. "Does this mean that I'm edging out tried-and-true Roger?"

She still hadn't told him that she'd broken up with Roger. Bridgette pressed her lips together to seal in the urge to confess. "Maybe."

He liked every part of her, but he preferred not talking to the back of her head. Blaine turned her around to face him. Knowing he was pushing it, he still couldn't resist asking, "Does he still live with the time lady?"

If smugness had a face, it was his. "Blaine—"

"I wondered what it would take to get you to say my name again." He drew her closer, tantalizing them both. The amusement in his eyes abated. "Listen, I just want you to know that I don't like treading on another man's territory."

He might look serious, but she wasn't buying it. Not for a minute. This man was a walking, breathing Romeo. Not a womanizer as Diane had insisted. Over the last few weeks,

Bridgette hadn't been able to discover anything remotely abusive or self-serving about him. But nonetheless, he wasn't the type to cleave the hearth and home, to tie himself down to one woman. He'd told her that his experience with Diane had taught him that married life wasn't for him. Once burnt, you didn't mess with a flame thrower. Meaning, she supposed, her.

"Yeah, right."

It bothered Blaine that she didn't believe him, but there was nothing he could do about it. Except state his case. "No, really. If I'd felt that you were really happy with Roger, I would have taken this feeling I have for you—"

"Lust?" she supplied archly, though in her heart, a secret part of her prayed that it wasn't.

"This *feeling*," he repeated more emphatically, "I have for you and would have tried to deal with it without messing up your life." Blaine looked into her eyes. The hell he would have left her alone. She'd gotten under his skin without either of them wanting it. "Well, maybe not, but I would have tried a little."

It was getting increasingly difficult to maintain this charade. Common sense told her to hang on to her shield while everything else told her to toss it aside and hang on to him, instead.

"What makes you think I'm not happy with Roger?" *Other than the fact that I haven't seen him in four weeks.*

That was easy. He brushed a stray strand of hair away from her temple. "Your eyes."

"My eyes," she repeated, mocking him. Of all the trite, clichéd—

"Your eyes," he echoed. "The way they look just after I kiss you. Just *before* I kiss you." They pulled him in, just as they were doing now. "A woman doesn't look like that if she's content with the man she's involved with." He smiled into her eyes. "Or says she's involved with."

He was getting too close to the truth. Bridgette drew away,

putting the length of the room between them as she resumed straightening it. "And you're an expert on this?"

He was right behind her, crowding her space. Crowding her soul. "Only takes one to make you an expert."

Blaine slid the back of his hand against her hair. Bridgette felt herself weakening, but she refused to face him, determined to hold her own.

"Let's just say, for the sake of argument, that you might, just *might*," she qualified, "have a point."

"Yes?"

She addressed her words to the lithograph on the opposite wall. Even that didn't help. She saw Blaine's face reflected there. Just the way it was inside her heart. Damn, it wasn't fair.

"It's something *I* have to deal with, not you." She picked up the pillow on the sofa and plumped it up again. "I'll let you know when it's all straightened out."

"Can I lobby?"

Bridgette turned around to look at him. "What?"

Blaine took the cushion out of her hands and dropped it on the sofa without looking. He moved into the space it had created between them.

"You know, lobby, like they do in Washington when a special interest group wants a bill to be passed." She didn't even notice it happening, but Blaine had her in his arms again. "Wine you, dine you, give you little bribes." His smile was less friendly than unnervingly sensual. "I'd really like to win this."

"'This'?" Her brows drew together. "As in contest? As in game?"

"As in everything," he breathed.

She knew what was coming next. Being braced for it didn't help. How could it when she was on his side? Before his mouth met hers, she was on her toes, arching into the kiss, anticipating the wild rush that was waiting for her.

Bridgette forgot all the other points she wanted to make, all the arguments she had so neatly at her disposal stating why she was against having this happen. Roger might not be part of the game plan anymore, but not getting hurt still was.

So why was she ruining everything by showing Blaine that what he surmised was really true?

Because she ceased to be a rational person when he kissed her. She became, just as Nonna had said, a woman given to passion.

She felt sinfully wonderful in his arms. Blaine knew if he continued kissing her, the last shred of common sense would evaporate from his brain and he'd push this further than he had a feeling she was willing to let it go for now.

If that wasn't enough of a deterrent, the fact that they were far from alone was. When he made love with her the first time, he didn't want it to be in the middle of a Boy Scout jamboree.

With an effort that would have made a ninja warrior proud, Blaine forced himself to draw away. His heart still pounding in his chest, he held her to him and took comfort in the feel of her body against his.

It was comforting, but far from soothing.

"You saved my life today," he murmured against her hair.

She smiled and he could feel her mouth curving against his chest. "All part of the service."

There was still a favor he had to ask her. Sometimes, being a coward had its advantages. "Speaking of which, would you like to continue saving my life?"

She raised her head to look at him. The boys were all in bed. "Exactly what did you have in mind?"

He fought back the urge to kiss her again. "Stay the night."

Her mouth fell open as disappointment filled her. How could he ask her to share his bed with a house full of children a room away? Indignant and upset that she'd misjudged him, that he could be like this, she pushed him away.

"And here I was, giving you points for being a good father."

Her eyes flashed with anger. "I can't stay here with you, you—" She was at a loss as to what to call him.

"You won't be staying with me," he interrupted mildly, his voice a direct contrast to hers, "you'll be staying with them. In a manner of speaking," he added.

She had no idea what he was talking about, only that some of the hot air had left her balloon. "To quote Mickey, 'huh?'"

Now that she was no longer scowling, Blaine allowed himself a grin. "Did you think I was asking you to stay for a night of incredible passion and lovemaking?"

He was having fun at her expense. But what else could she have thought? She had momentarily lost sight of whom she was dealing with. "You just answered the question yourself."

He toyed with her hair. Bridgette jerked her head back, her eyes demanding an explanation.

"Not that I wouldn't want that more than I want to wake up tomorrow morning, but in case you haven't noticed, there's a house full of kids to act as chaperon, even if we didn't count Jack."

Her expression told him what she thought of Jack acting as chaperon. "Jack told us he was deaf and blind last week and was offering to sleep with a pillow over his head," she reminded him, not that, she thought, he needed reminding. "I don't think keeping us apart is uppermost in his mind."

Blaine ran his palms along her bare arms, fantasizing about what it would be like to do the same along all of her. Another time. "It isn't in mine, either, but there are certain sacrifices a father has to make."

He looked as if he were actually serious, she thought. Maybe she had overreacted a little. Again. Some things were hard to get over. "I'm impressed."

The sarcastic edge was missing from her voice. He took it as a good sign.

"Good, this may work out to my benefit after all." Surprising her, Blaine pressed a quick kiss to her neck. It had the desired effect. Her eyes were smoky. "This isn't over, merely postponed," he promised softly along her skin. "You can have the master bedroom. The sofa—" he glanced at it, remembering the eager jumpers he'd herded away "—if it still works, opens up. I can sleep out here." Though the prospect wasn't heartening.

It still didn't make any sense to her. "Why do you want me to stay? They're sleeping."

He'd learned to be very leery in the last few hours. "But for how long?"

The boys had spent so much energy playing, she didn't think any of them would be up before the morning. "You're doing just fine."

Blaine shook his head. Some risks he wasn't willing to take just yet. Murphy's Law had an ugly habit of rearing its head when least expected.

"I've walked across the tightrope, but I'm not ready to take away the safety net just yet. Not with a horde of kids, anyway." He gave her his most encouraging smile. "And you're so good with them."

If he shoveled it any deeper… "Is this how you coax petulant models into working?"

He grinned at her, knowing he'd won. Maybe he'd get a decent night's sleep after all. "I don't know. Are you being petulant?"

She laughed, then shook her head. She was wavering, but the debate was still alive in her mind. "I didn't bring anything with me to sleep in."

"Please." Blaine clutched at his heart dramatically. "I can only restrain myself for so long." When she hit him, he volunteered, "I guess you can wear one of my T-shirts as a nightshirt." He felt a warmth spreading through him as he envisioned it. "After which, I'll probably wear it close to my heart for a week."

She couldn't help the laugh that bubbled up. "You're crazy, you know that?"

"Yeah, I guess I am." His eyes caressed her mouth just before his lips did. "About you." He smiled at her, a genuine, heart-felt smile. "Thanks for staying."

She raised a hand in protest, though it was halfhearted. "I didn't say yes, yet."

"But you will." He took her into his arms again, linking his fingers around her waist loosely. "You have a weakness for underdogs."

She arched her brow. "You, Blaine O'Connor, are far from an underdog."

When she looked like that, he found it hard to think of anything but undressing her, of making slow, languid love to every part of her. "Someday, when the house isn't full of kids and a coughing, retired policeman, I'll show you just how far."

Bridgette heard the desire in his voice and felt something stirring in kind within her. She was very grateful for the house full of kids and coughing, retired policeman. Otherwise, mistakes might be made. And hearts might be lost. Mainly hers.

She bit her lip, debating. It was late and she supposed it wouldn't hurt if she remained for the night. Blaine did look a little uneasy about the prospect of having to handle by himself any emergency that might arise. And it would all be perfectly proper. Probably more proper than she wanted, if she was being honest with herself.

Bridgette sighed, surrendering, though she wasn't altogether pleased that he was so sure of her. "Oh, all right."

He laughed and hugged her to him quickly before releasing her. "Knew I could count on you."

"Don't get too cocky," she warned, knowing that he would and with reason. "This is for Mickey."

"I know," he assured her a bit too solemnly. "I can still be grateful." He gestured toward the telephone in the kitchen, even though there was one in the master bedroom. "Is there anyone you want to call first? Like the time lady?"

She shot him a warning look. "Don't make me regret this. I do have to call Nonna. She tends to worry when I don't come home."

That was something he'd been wondering about. "Why do you still live at home, if you don't mind my asking?"

She supposed that to some, it might seem unusual. But it suited her.

"I was in a car accident a couple of years ago. When I was released from the hospital, Nonna insisted I stay with her and Gino." Bridgette raised her hand, stopping him before he had a chance to ask. "Gino moved back home when he decided to go to med school. It's cheaper. Anyway, she nursed me until I got back on my feet. I had a lot of time to think while I was lying there. I decided to get that education I was always putting off. So I went back to school for my master's. Living with Nonna made things easier. Also less expensive. Besides—" she shrugged, making no apologies for the way she felt "—I really enjoy being around her. She seems to light up every day."

The way, he thought, she did his. "Must be a family thing."

He was getting to her. "I'd better turn in." With legs that felt just the slightest bit wooden, she began to move toward the threshold of the bedroom. If she didn't go soon, she knew she never would.

He nodded, then called after her. "Oh, one more thing."

Bridgette stopped short of the hallway and turned. "Yes?"

Blaine grinned, but his eyes were serious. "Lock your door. I'm not completely sure how long this noble thing can last."

She smiled, belying the fact that her heart had sped up to double time. He knew just how to get to her! "Gino taught me a few self-defense moves. I don't think you have to worry about sullying my virtue."

Even being flipped by her sounded inviting right now. "That's comforting to know."

Bridgette crossed back to him quickly and brushed a soft kiss along his cheek. When he looked at her in surprise, she said, "You did good tonight."

He slid his fingertips along his cheek, as if he could feel the impression of her lips. "Thanks, Teach."

"Don't mention it."

Bridgette hurried away, afraid that if she lingered one more moment, she'd give in to an urge that was growing at a rapid rate, threatening to consume her and any noble intentions that Blaine might have left.

He woke up to muted, distant noise.

Accustomed to waking up in strange beds in strange hotel rooms, it took Blaine only a moment to orient himself after he opened his eyes. The noise, he ascertained, was coming from the kitchen.

The next moment, the scent of coffee mingling with bacon had him sitting up. He always woke up hungry. Had Jack gotten better and come down? He found that explanation unlikely.

Bridgette.

An image of her, wearing only his T-shirt—the one that had shrunk in the last wash—flashed alluringly through his sleepy brain. Blaine stumbled off the convertible sofa. A sheet dragged behind him the first few steps until he shook it off. Rubbing the sleep from his eyes in a manner that was completely reminiscent of his son, Blaine made his way into the kitchen.

He was disappointed.

"You're dressed," he lamented as he sat down on the nearest stool at the breakfast nook counter.

"Sorry about that." There was mischief in her eyes. "I didn't think standing here in a T-shirt and nothing else was exactly appropriate. This is a G-rated breakfast."

Her hair was piled haphazardly up on her head. The ends

were still damp from a quick shower. If Blaine leaned forward, he could smell his soap on her. Seven in the morning was too early to drive himself crazy like this.

Bridgette was oblivious to what he was going through. Her mind was on toast. "I thought I'd take a tray up to Jack and then feed the boys." She deposited the last of the eggs into the pan. "Want to pitch in, or watch?"

He stole a piece of bacon from the drainer. "My expertise ends with 'Pass the mayo.'"

Bridgette looked at him in surprise. He'd lived alone for so long. "You don't cook?"

He had never felt the need to go through the trouble of learning. "The world is full of restaurants and take-out places."

"Not to mention willing women."

Blaine grinned, munching. "In a pinch, I can make a sandwich or butter some toast."

She laughed, shaking her head. "You're hopeless. Even Gino cooks." Nonna had made it a point to teach both of them while they were still very young.

Blaine propped his head up on his upturned palm as he watched her move about the kitchen, the picture of sexy domesticity, even if she wasn't wearing his T-shirt. "You could teach me."

Who was he kidding? The only thing he felt like cooking with was her. The toaster popped behind her and she took out four slices, feeding four more into it. "I'll put it on my list of things to do."

"Do that." He glanced at the three pans spread out on the stove. Bacon was frying in the largest pan. The other two contained scrambled eggs.

"I thought eggs were supposed to be bad for you." Not that it had ever stopped him. Bacon and eggs were his favorite breakfast.

She swatted his hand away from the drainer, aborting his attempt to steal another piece of bacon. "Once in a while doesn't hurt. Besides, those are mostly egg whites. Toss in a few yokes," she explained, "and the kids don't notice."

He thought of last night's feeding frenzy. "Those kids wouldn't notice if you tossed in a few worms." Blaine glanced at the stacked empty pizza boxes near the door. He'd have to get to that right after he ate. "I think they'd eat anything."

Bridgette arranged a covered plate of eggs and toast, coffee and a glass of juice on the tray she'd found in one of the lower cupboards. "That makes my job that much less difficult." Finished, she picked up the tray and began walking out the doorway.

Blaine slid off the stool quickly and took the tray out of her hands. If there was to be a division of labor, he knew which task he wanted to be assigned. "Here, I'll take that to Jack, you deal with the horde."

She laughed at his description. "Coward."

He saw no reason to deny the obvious. "That's me." He kissed her lips quickly, knowing that to do anything else would mean abandoning the tray altogether. And the boys would be up soon. "You look great in the morning."

She smiled at the compliment, knowing it probably meant nothing to him.

His hair was in his eyes, which still had a sleepy cast to them. Blaine was bare-chested and in his cutoffs. The image was an unsettling one, but she held on to the impression his face made. "And you look like a little boy."

He'd seen the way she'd looked at him when he'd first walked in. No one eyed a little boy that way. But he played along, letting her have it her way. "Is that good, or bad?"

He already knew the answer to that. She could tell by his self-assured grin. Bridgette waved him out the door. "Just take the tray upstairs."

"It's good," he crowed. "I knew it."

She had no doubts that he'd known it all along. With a shake of her head, Bridgette went to get Mickey and the others.

* * *

When Blaine returned downstairs, he found them all seated around the dining room table, an equal number of boys flanking Bridgette on either side. There was a place set for him at the head of the table, but he stood in the doorway for a moment, absorbing the scene.

Bridgette looked up, wondering why he wasn't eating. He certainly couldn't have filled up on the pieces of bacon he'd stolen. There was an odd look on his face. If she didn't know any better, she would have called it contentment.

"Something wrong?"

He shook his head. No, everything was right, he realized. Very right. He indicated the table and its occupants. "I think Norman Rockwell painted this for one of his magazine covers."

Bridgette looked around at the boys. Most of them were completely involved in the business of polishing off their plates. They looked none the worse for their long night. She sensed that once they'd had their fill, they'd be looking for something new to get into. She had to admit, although silently, that she was relieved that the slumber party was almost over.

"Well, it certainly isn't still life, I'll give you that."

Blaine seated himself and looked at her across the table. "What else can you give me?"

Bridgette pinned him with a warning look. "A bill for services rendered if you don't wipe that smile off your face."

Mickey stopped eating. He looked from his father to Bridgette, curious. "Why should he wipe it off, Bridgette? Don't you like my dad smiling?"

Yes, very much. She deliberately looked away from Blaine's amused expression. "Remind me to explain that to you when you get older." She rose, her plate in her hand. "Anyone want seconds?"

Hands shot up all around the table like jackknives being pressed into service.

Blaine could only marvel. If *he* had asked, there would have been a stampede into the kitchen. "Just like in school. How *do* you do that?"

She looked at him smugly before retreating to the kitchen. "It's a gift."

By eight-thirty, parents began arriving to pick up their sons. Bridgette joined Mickey at the door to say goodbye to each boy as he left. Each one held a party bag filled with small prizes and reminders of the party. Another thing he wouldn't have thought of, Blaine mused as he watched Bridgette with his son.

It occurred to him that they looked very good together. He both liked the idea and felt a little intimidated by it. "I'll just go and look in on Jack," he said after the last child had gone.

Mickey conspicuously waited until Blaine left the room before turning to Bridgette. "It was the best party ever, Bridgette. Thanks."

She was touched. They'd gone through the forest and were seeing the light on the other side. But she also realized that Mickey was saying it to her, not to Blaine. That wasn't going to work.

"I'm glad you enjoyed it. But you know, your dad had a lot to do with it."

Mickey shrugged as they walked away from the door. "That's because you made him."

She draped her arm around his shoulders. At five two, she wasn't that much taller than he was. He'd outgrow her in another year, she mused.

"No, he wanted to, Mickey. He just didn't really know how." Blaine and Mickey were two kind, good people, fumbling at being a family. "You've got to help him along with this. He loves you a great deal. We both do." She looked into his face, searching it intently for a sign. "You do believe that, don't you?"

Mickey nodded. The action was no longer mechanical. "Yes, I guess I do."

His response wasn't enough. "There's no guesswork involved, Mickey. It's a simple fact." Enough lecturing. "And now, since all your friends are gone, I want to be able to hug the birthday boy."

She waited for permission. This was a very narrow path she'd burrowed through in the snow. She didn't want to risk having an avalanche fall, covering it again.

"Is that all right with you?"

He shifted from foot to foot as he shrugged. "It's not my birthday anymore."

"We'll pretend." But she made no move to hug him. "Is it all right?"

"Yeah, sure."

Only then did she hug him tightly to her. And only for a moment. There was no need to abuse a newly awarded privilege. Mickey was a little stiff at first, but he gradually melted into the hug.

Yes, she thought, a definite light at the end of the forest.

Chapter Eleven

She had been the epitome of mysteriousness. Nonna, who, as she enthusiastically forged through the world, would blissfully announce every last detail of her life, had finally managed to keep something a secret.

And it was driving Bridgette crazy.

It began abruptly with Nonna's announcement that she was throwing a party Saturday afternoon—a party, she had hinted, with a very specific purpose. But when Bridgette asked her what it was, Nonna only smiled and remained silent.

Most people were predictable. But since the only predictable thing about Nonna was that she was unpredictable, Bridgette was at a loss as to where this was all heading.

She'd gotten nothing more out of Nonna right up to the moment that the guests began arriving.

"Why can't you tell me?" Bridgette pressed. "You've always told me everything."

Nonna waved a greeting at a couple Gino had just admitted. "Almost everything, Brita," she corrected. Amusement mingled with mischief and fairly gleamed in her eyes. "Besides, I will tell you, once everyone has arrived."

Gino seated himself at the piano and began to play, which meant, Bridgette thought, that he had silently relegated the job of opening the door for the arriving guests to her. It figured. But she had too many other things on her mind to waste time being annoyed with him. How could Nonna keep something from her?

"Do you mean that after all these years, I don't get preferential treatment?"

Nonna cupped Bridgette's chin in her hand and laughed softly. "I have always preferred you, *bella*. But for now, let me have my fun. Besides," she was unable to resist adding, "if you think about it, I know it will come to you before the others."

She looked toward Jack and sighed like a woman enjoying a fantasy. Or a dream. Like a woman, Bridgette thought enviously, who was loved and in love.

Nonna was edging away to join Jack at the piano. In parting, she gave Bridgette one last hint. "It goes along with our little midnight talk. The last one, over rum-and-raisin."

"We talked about Blaine and Roger." And very little had gotten resolved since then, she added silently.

The same secretive smile she'd worn all week lifted the corners of Sophia's mouth.

"Think," she prodded, linking hands with Jack. "We talked of something bigger than that."

The doorbell rang, robbing Bridgette of any further opportunity to grill Nonna.

Maybe Nonna and Jack were going away together, she thought as she crossed to the door. Gino was playing a love song. Maybe he was on to something.

Bridgette opened the door and a smile instantly materialized. "Hi."

Blaine and Mickey were standing on her doorstep. Blaine was wearing a navy blue sports jacket and gray slacks. She'd never seen him in anything but jeans and pullovers before. The contrast was stunning. She could see why Diane's mind had worked overtime.

Mickey was wearing a dark blue suit, and while he looked handsome, he also looked utterly uncomfortable in the clothes.

Blaine brushed a quick kiss on her lips before she had the chance to protest. "So, what's the big secret?" He ushered Mickey in.

She shut the door slowly, wondering if she would ever get to the point where she was unaffected by him. She strongly doubted it, even if she was given the opportunity, which she knew she wouldn't be.

"Nonna wouldn't tell me." She didn't enjoy admitting that. It made her feel like an outsider. "I'm just as much in the dark as you are." She looked at Mickey. Even at his age, he had the makings of a heartbreaker. Like his father, she thought. "Hi, Mickey. I'm so glad you could make it."

Mickey wasn't about to take any undue credit. "Dad brought me."

She smoothed down the upturned portion of his collar. "Does that mean you didn't want to come?"

He hadn't meant to hurt Bridgette's feelings. It was only the suit he minded, not the fact that he had to be here. "No, I wanted to come."

"Good." She hooked an arm through Mickey's and began to lead him into the living room. "Well, now that my two favorite guys are here—"

Blaine fell into step on her other side. "Thanks."

Bridgette lifted her chin. "I wasn't referring to you."

The smile on Blaine's face told her that he didn't believe her. He looked around the room. There were a few people he knew. Jack's friends. "Where *is* Roger?" he asked innocently.

She wasn't about to go into that now. "I was referring to Jack," she improvised as if he hadn't said anything.

For Mickey's benefit, she nodded toward Jack, who was on the far side of the piano. He had his arm around Nonna's waist and they had their heads together as they listened to Gino play.

They look like two teenagers from here, she thought.

"Then Roger isn't here?"

Blaine's question brought her attention back to him. "No." She bit off the word.

"Is he coming?"

She paused a moment, summoning patience before answering. "No."

"Why not?"

She knew she couldn't hit him. There were too many witnesses.

There was a wealth of excuses she could give him. Several presented themselves to her spontaneously as she stood there. But her heart wasn't in it. Bridgette didn't want to lie about Roger. There was no reason for it anymore.

Over the last two months, Blaine and Mickey had made great headway in redefining the bond that had been abruptly thrown into upheaval with Diane's death. After a shaky start, Blaine was finally becoming a real father to the boy in every sense of the word. Bridgette no longer had any moral obligation, real or imagined, to oversee Blaine's every move.

That meant she wouldn't be in the picture much anymore. If Blaine didn't feel that he needed her help, he would move on to someone more his style. Someone more suited to a casual relationship. He'd never given her any indication that he wanted anything else from her but a casual relationship, one with no strings. And there was nothing about her, she knew, that was casual. She was intense and she needed to feel that sort of intensity in return.

What she needed, she knew, was a commitment.

Blaine was committed to his son and his work. That much was plain, and there was no space left over. There was no use in thinking she could burrow in. She didn't want to burrow in just for a limited time.

She wanted forever.

Bridgette shrugged in reply to his question as Gino began to play "Moon River." "He's not here because I didn't invite him."

Blaine was just getting warmed up. He already had his answer. He and Jack had had a long talk last night about a variety of topics. Bridgette and Roger had been one of them.

But he wanted *her* to tell him why Roger wasn't here. Why he wasn't part of her life. It was, Blaine thought, part of setting the stage for the final act. A final act he'd hope to pull off. "And why is that?"

Damn him, why did he have to keep prodding like this? "Because we're not—"

She broke off as Mickey bolted from the room. It took her a minute to connect his flight with the song that Gino was playing.

"Oh, God, Diane used to sing that to Mickey when she put him to bed. He always begged her for it. He even has a worn-out copy of it somewhere." Upset, she hurried after Mickey. But Blaine caught her wrist, restraining her.

"It's okay. I'll handle this."

Blaine had no idea what he was going to say to Mickey. He only knew that he had to say something. His son was hurting and he needed him.

Numbed, Bridgette nodded and stepped back. Emotions tumbled about within her like clothes chasing one another in a dryer as she watched Blaine go after Mickey. She wanted to comfort Mickey herself, but she knew that Blaine was right. It was to him that Mickey needed to turn, not her. Hadn't she maintained all along that Blaine was the one who was supposed to make an effort to mend the breach with his son? That it was Blaine's responsibility to give his son emotional support?

He was finally doing it. So why did she feel so left out?

She tried to concentrate on the good she'd accomplished and

not dwell on what it meant to her personally. Blaine had changed, grown. He wasn't hiding behind excuses anymore and shirking his responsibility as a father. He hadn't just waved a hand at Mickey and mumbled that he would get over it, the way her own father would have.

Blaine had graduated.

A bittersweet smile played on her lips. Blaine didn't need a teacher anymore. His parenting instincts had finally kicked in.

There was only one thing left for her to do. Bridgette went to tell Gino to stop playing "Moon River" and play something else.

Blaine hurried down the hall, looking into the rooms as he passed. Mickey wasn't in any of them. The boy wasn't anywhere to be seen.

Where had he gotten off to?

He reached the end of the house. Beyond the family room was the patio, but it appeared to be empty. Blaine was about to retrace his steps when he saw the drape at the window moving slightly, as if the wind were ruffling it.

Except that the windows were all closed.

"Mickey?" he called softly as he crossed to the drape. There was no answer.

Blaine drew the gray fabric aside slowly. Mickey was huddled behind it. His face was turned to the window, his shoulders hunched and shaking.

Mickey was crying.

"Go away," he mumbled, embarrassment and anger mingling in the plea.

Blaine gently placed his hands on the boy's shoulders. "Mickey, you're my son. I'm not going away."

Mickey wanted to die, to fold up until he disappeared altogether. "But I'm crying. I don't want you to see me cry."

His son was desperately trying to get him to go away, but he wasn't about to leave. Not anymore. Not ever again.

"There's nothing wrong with crying, Mickey." Blaine took the boy into his arms. Mickey was stiff, awkward with the feeling that had overpowered him. "Crying helps you get rid of all those sad feelings you've been keeping locked inside."

Once they started, Mickey couldn't stop the flow of tears. It was as if something had ripped open inside of him. Only a moment before, he'd tried to push him away. Now he clung to his father as if he were afraid of being blown away by the fierceness of the emotion he'd unleashed.

Blaine held Mickey tightly against him. He stroked the boy's head, wishing he was as good as Bridgette in a situation like that. Blaine felt ill-equipped, but at least he could offer Mickey his love.

"I was beginning to worry about you, you know," he told the boy after a few moments. "Grandpa said you didn't cry at the funeral."

"I thought she was going to come back."

Stunned, Blaine looked down at the boy huddled against him. "Why?"

"Because I wished for it." His voice was thick with unshed tears. "At my party, when I blew out the candles. I wished for it."

"Oh, Mickey." Blaine thought his own heart would break. "She's not coming back," he said softly.

"I know." Mickey's sobs began to abate slowly. "I miss her, Dad. I miss Mom something awful." At the admission, fresh tears sprang to his eyes. "I thought, maybe, if I didn't cry, the hurt would go away. But it didn't. It just sat there, right in my chest, like a rock. I couldn't even breathe without it hurting."

Blaine had felt the same way about his own parents' passing. And he'd been a great deal older than Mickey at the time. How much harder was it to face when you were only Mickey's age?

"I know, son, I know." He wanted to tell Mickey that everything would be all right, that it would be just as it used to be, but to lie to him would be unfair. "Eventually, that rock'll get smaller, but it's never going to go away entirely. It'll always be there to remind you." Blaine paused for a moment, searching for a way to temper that stark reality somehow. "And maybe that's good in a way, because you don't ever want to forget your mother."

He felt Mickey's arms tighten around him. "Do you miss her, too?"

Blaine thought of the woman he had fallen in love with, the young woman, barely out of her teens, who had made him feel as if he'd been the first one to discover this wondrous sensation. He separated the memory from the woman that jealousy and insecurity had caused her to become.

"Yes, Mickey, I miss her, too."

Mickey looked up at his father, blinking back his tears. They shimmered on his lashes like tiny crystals. Somehow, it made all the difference in the world to him to know that he could share this feeling, his pain, with his father.

He sniffled, attempting to drain himself of any more tears. "I love you, Dad."

Blaine's heart swelled. He couldn't remember Mickey ever saying that to him.

"I love you, too, Mickey." Blaine felt his throat choke with emotion. "Very, very much." He reached into his pocket and took out a handkerchief, then passed it to his son. "Do you want to go back to the party? Bridgette looked pretty worried when you took off."

Mickey blew once into the handkerchief, then offered it back to his father. "I don't want her to worry. She's really great."

Blaine slipped the handkerchief back into his pocket as he smiled at his son's assessment. "Yes, she is."

Something else they could share, Mickey thought. The idea brightened him. He looked up at his father, studying him. "You really like her?"

"Yes, I really like her." They began to return to the living room, and then Blaine paused. "Mickey, hold on a minute. I want to talk to you before we go back. Man to man."

Mickey wiped away the last telltale streak from his chin and grinned up at his father. He liked the sound of that, liked being thought of as an equal.

"Sure."

What was taking them so long?

It was all Bridgette could do to keep from going after them. It had been at least five minutes, if not more, since Blaine had disappeared in Mickey's wake, and her patience was giving way fast.

Not to mention the fact that she felt completely shut out.

First Nonna wouldn't confide in her about her secret, then Blaine and Mickey were forming a bond without her. It was exactly what she'd wanted for both of them, but she couldn't help being a little sad. Bridgette felt like a child looking into a toy store window at Christmas, wistfully watching other children walk off with toys that she coveted.

With treasures she wanted to play with.

Anxiously, she watched the entrance to the living room, mentally giving them three more minutes. After that, she was butting in.

She could tell as soon as they entered that everything had gone well. Blaine had his hand draped on Mickey's shoulders and they were talking amicably. Mickey was actually laughing.

No, she thought ruefully, they certainly didn't need her anymore.

This must have been what a mother bird felt like after she had pushed the last small occupant out of the nest and watched it soar. Proud, happy and lonely at the same time. All she needed, Bridgette mused, was feathers to complete the comparison.

She bit her lower lip, getting her remorse under control before she made her way over to them. This was no time for regrets. Mickey was happy, that was all that mattered.

Bridgette looked from father to son as she reached them. "Everything all right?"

"Everything's fine," Mickey volunteered.

His eyes were dancing, she thought, literally dancing. Whatever Blaine had said to him had obviously worked miracles. Curious, she leveled a quizzical glance at Blaine.

"Fine," he echoed.

His arm still on his shoulders, Blaine hugged Mickey to him. It was a small, fleeting gesture, but Mickey received it without flinching or squirming. It spoke volumes.

Blaine dropped his arm, then looked at Bridgette. "Now then, you were saying—?"

Oh, no, not again. The man had a mind like a pit bull once he latched on to something.

"Nothing important," she retorted, fervently wishing he'd drop the subject.

Maybe she would resurrect her relationship with Roger, at least as far as Blaine was concerned. This way, she'd have an excuse and a way to save face as she eased out of their lives.

"No, I want to hear," Blaine coaxed. "Why didn't you invite Roger?"

Was it her imagination, or was Mickey actually struggling to keep a straight face? She looked from the boy to Blaine, wondering what was going on.

For the second time in the space of a few minutes, any answer she might have made was interrupted. Jack was in the center of the room by the baby grand, calling for attention.

He rapped a spoon against his wineglass. "Everyone, I have an announcement to make."

Out of the corner of her eye, Bridgette saw Blaine and Mickey exchange knowing looks.

"You know?" she whispered in surprise. He'd just asked her if she knew what was going on when he had come in.

Blaine nodded, picking up two glasses from a nearby table. He handed one to Bridgette.

So this was something they were going to be toasting, she thought. "How?"

Blaine handed Mickey a glass of ginger ale. The boy accepted it and Bridgette saw his chest puff up. "Jack can't keep a secret."

He was doing this to her intentionally, she thought. Keeping the secret from her. "What is it?"

Blaine wasn't about to spoil the moment for Sophia and Jack. He gestured toward the couple with his glass. Jack was waiting for everyone to settle down.

"Shh," Blaine chided. He was obviously enjoying himself at her expense, Bridgette thought. "Listen."

Surrounded by a ring of their friends, Jack stepped forward. His hand was linked with Nonna's. They looked every bit as young, Bridgette thought, as the couple she'd seen photographed on the society page this morning.

And then it came to her.

She'd been so wound up with Mickey and Blaine and her own feelings that she hadn't noticed much of anything else. If she had, she would have put this together long before today.

The lines that time and experience had etched into Jack's face deepened as he smiled at the gathering.

"It's not often that an old war-horse like me gets a second opportunity to find the perfect woman." He paused as he looked at the woman beside him. It was the first time Bridgette could remember ever seeing Nonna blush. "But in this case, lightning struck twice. I found Sophia Rafanelli."

Sophia bowed graciously, her eyes shining with amusement. And love. Bridgette could see it even from where she stood.

A smattering of applause met Jack's statement. He held his free hand up to postpone it until he was finished. "And even though she's a smart little cookie, she still said yes when I asked her to marry me."

"I know a good deal when I see one," Nonna told the circle of people crowding around them. She had to raise her voice to be heard above the swell of voices congratulating them.

Mickey tugged on his father's arm, a thought suddenly occurring to him.

"Does that mean that she's going to be my grandmother now? Officially?" He had taken an instant liking to the older woman the first time he'd met her. The idea that they were going to be related pleased him.

Blaine easily read Mickey's thoughts. "It sure does."

Mickey paused for a moment, digesting the connection and the possible repercussions that had. He glanced at Bridgette. "Does that make Bridgette your sister?"

"I sure hope not."

Bridgette had no time to savor the implication or the lusty laugh that accompanied Blaine's comment. It wafted after her like a seductive melody as she made her way to her grandmother's side.

She pretended that she was offended but couldn't quite carry it off. "You didn't tell me."

Like an entertainer pleased with her audience's reaction, Sophia laughed and hugged Bridgette to her. "I wanted to surprise you. I see that I did." She held the girl she had loved and guided from scraped knees to womanhood. "Be happy for me, Brita?"

"You know I am." Bridgette hugged her grandmother again. For as long as she could remember, Nonna had taken life's curves alone, fending for her and Gino. Bridgette had never known her grandfather. He'd died a year before she was born. It was time that Nonna had a little special love of her own in her life.

Releasing Nonna, Bridgette turned toward Jack and was enfolded in a bear hug.

"I'm not sure I can forgive you." When he raised a brow at her comment, she accused. "You told Blaine."

"I had to." Jack laughed as he linked his hand with Sophia's again. "He threatened to torture me. But he promised not to tell anyone else."

Blaine had been too closemouthed for her liking. Had the tables been turned, she would have told him.... Well, she amended silently, glancing at Nonna, maybe not.

"He kept his word." It was going to be a struggle to get accustomed to thinking of Nonna as a married woman. But it was an adjustment she was looking forward to making. "I'm thrilled for both of you."

"You know that goes double for me," Gino told them as he draped an arm casually over Bridgette's shoulder.

She gave him a look that was usually reserved for siblings. In their case, it fit. "You always were competitive."

"No," Gino teased. "You were. I was always the standard you had to measure up to."

"Ha! You wish."

Jack winked at Sophia. "Makes me glad we're too old to have kids."

Sophia raised her chin exactly the way Bridgette was wont to. "Speak for yourself."

Tickled, Jack laughed. "My mistake. Hey, everybody, I've got the youngest woman here." He planted a kiss on her cheek.

"You will have to do better than that to atone, old man." Taking his face between her hands, Sophia kissed Jack soundly on the mouth. Applause and catcalls greeted her action as Jack pretended to grow weak in the knees.

"As a wedding present," Gino interjected when the noise died down, "I'm moving out. I've finally found a studio apartment near the hospital I can afford. Now I won't have so far to commute. You two lovebirds can cavort around the house to your hearts' content." Glancing at Bridgette, he bit his tongue. He'd forgotten about her. "I mean—"

Bridgette was quick to sail into the opening. "I guess it's

time for me to tell you. I'm moving out, too." She saw the surprised look on Nonna's face and hastily continued, "I've almost got my degree, and it's time I was out of your hair. I didn't want to mention it before it was all settled, but now that it is, it all seems to have worked out rather neatly, don't you think?"

Sophia looked at her doubtfully. Bridgette usually told her everything. Though Bridgette was certainly a grown woman who had lived on her own before, this move was an unexpected one.

"Are you sure, Brita? There is no hurry. Jack and I—"

She didn't want to give Nonna an opportunity to quiz her. "The landlord might disagree with you. I've signed the lease and everything." It wasn't going to be easy, she thought, scrambling for a place to move into quickly, but she could manage. The last thing she wanted was to be in the way.

Bridgette kissed each on the cheek, then picked up her wineglass. "So, once again, congratulations, you two, and may all your fights end in an embrace."

Jack waved away the wish as unnecessary. "We don't fight."

Bridgette gave him a knowing smile. "That's because Nonna's been on her best behavior. Give it a while, trust me."

Laughing, Nonna took a playful swing at Bridgette. Reacting, Bridgette moved out of her grandmother's reach. She collided with Blaine, who'd come up behind her to extend his own wishes. As she stumbled and tried to regain her balance, the champagne in her glass went flying onto his shirt.

"Hey!" The liquid felt cold as it made contact with his skin. "I've already been baptized once." He tried to brush the champagne away and only succeeded in rubbing it in, instead.

"Oh, I'm sorry." Setting the glass down on a table, she frowned at the mess. "C'mon, I'll get a towel and mop you up."

"I was under the impression that you could do that without resorting to a towel." Blaine grinned at the look she shot him.

He paused only to glance over his shoulder at Mickey. The

boy was occupied, talking to Gino. The latter was showing him some intricate fingering on the piano. Satisfied that he wouldn't be missed, Blaine followed Bridgette out of the room.

Chapter Twelve

Bridgette led the way into the small powder room that was off the side of the living room. Taking one of the small, fluffy pink towels that Nonna always put out for guests, she turned on the tap water and passed a corner of the towel under it.

Undoing one button on Blaine's shirt, she slipped her hand beneath the fabric. His skin felt warm against the back of her hand, and she had to struggle to concentrate on what she was doing. With determination, she began to wipe the stain with the towel.

His stomach muscles tightened as her knuckles lightly grazed his chest. "Hmm, this could get interesting."

Bridgette continued rubbing and didn't bother looking up. "Hold still."

The line between her brows deepened, as if she were a surgeon contemplating a difficult operating procedure. Blaine's mouth curved in a smile as he watched her. "Will I live, doctor?"

She raised her eyes to his, her fingers still busy. "A long and eventful life."

"That remains to be seen."

She wondered what he meant by that, but knew it was safer not to ask.

He didn't care about the stain. He wanted to take her into his arms, to hold her. His life was finally getting on the right track and he wanted her there to enjoy it with him. But for the moment, he let her work.

"Great news about Jack and Sophia, isn't it?" he began, looking for an opening.

"Yes, it is." An enigmatic smile slipped over her lips. "But I haven't forgiven you yet for not telling me."

Unable to take it anymore, he stopped her hands and tossed aside the towel. "It was his moment—I didn't want to steal his thunder."

Just exactly what did he think of her? Didn't he credit her with having the same sensitivity as he did? "I wouldn't have announced it at the door when everyone arrived."

He grinned. "You wouldn't have had to." Blaine cupped her chin in his hand. "Your face would have given you away. It's a very expressive face." And a dazzling one, he thought. One that haunted his nights. As well as his heart.

Bridgette pulled her head back. "Leave my face alone."

Blaine shook his head. Undaunted, he framed her face again, his fingers curving along the planes of her cheeks. He saw the reaction he wanted in her eyes. They'd grown large and smoky.

"I can't. Just like I can't leave the rest of you alone." He allowed his fingers to linger a moment longer before dropping his hands. He wanted to talk to her and he didn't want to distract himself. Touching her was a major distraction. He thought of what she'd told Sophia and Jack at the party. "You don't have a place to go, do you?"

She looked at him in surprise. "How did you—?" Bridgette realized that she was admitting it and made a stab at a recovery. "What makes you say that?"

"Your face again." He grinned engagingly as she scowled. "It's like an open book."

That meant he was telling her that he also knew how she felt about him. Bridgette didn't like the idea of being transparent.

"The library's closed." Her eyes cool, she glanced at the shirt. "There, I think we saved it." She turned to leave the small confinement.

He laid a hand on her shoulder and she stopped. "I can always buy another shirt."

Bridgette turned, her eyes snapping. "Good for you."

Did she have any idea how desirable she looked, her eyes flashing like blue flames against a darkened sky? He was going to enjoy showing her. Over and over again. "How about mine?"

She didn't understand. "Your shirt?"

He laughed. "My house. You need a place to stay. How about mine?"

She'd heard a lot more seductive propositions in her time, even if they had all been on television. The least he could have done was ask her after a night out. "You're asking me to move in with you?"

As far as he was concerned, she was already an integral part of his life. "You might say that."

What was he thinking of? Here she was, mentally patting him on the back, thrusting him into a tassel and gown, thinking he'd made the grade as a father and here he was asking her to do something that could make a terrible impression on his son.

"What about Mickey?"

That was the best part, he thought, reaching for her. "He wants you to move in, too. I checked."

She swatted his hand away and stared at him. Bridgette had wanted them to bond like a father and son, not like two carousing buddies. Obviously Blaine had missed a step here. "You *told* him about this?"

Why was she looking at him as if he had just sprung two heads and neither one matched the third?

"Yes."

Bridgette couldn't believe it. "About the fact that you wanted us to live together?"

He still didn't understand her reaction. Blaine replayed their conversation in his head. What was she getting so excited about? "Yes."

The very idea that he would have such a discussion with his son took her breath away. Mickey was eleven, not eighteen!

"How *could* you?"

Now he *knew* he must have missed a step somehow. "Weren't you the one who said I was supposed to talk to him about things?"

"Yes, but—"

He wasn't going to let her start sputtering again. He knew where that could lead. "And since we were going to be a family, if you agreed, I thought I should let him feel that he had a part in this. I don't see what's so wrong with that."

She held up her hand, her head beginning to spin. "Wait minute—"

A hesitant knock on the doorjamb interrupted anything she had to say. Bridgette flushed, realizing that they were being overheard. The door was open.

A statuesque woman wearing a red dress that amply accentuated the difference between men and women was standing in the doorway. She smiled at Blaine. "Would you mind? I need to powder my nose."

Bridgette didn't recognize her. She vaguely remembered Nonna saying that one of Jack's friends was bringing his daughter.

Obviously all daughters were not created equal.

"Sure, sorry." Bridgette stepped out of the woman's way. Blaine, she suddenly realized, didn't even give the woman a second glance. Maybe there was some hope, after all.

"It's all yours," Blaine told the woman.

He took Bridgette's hand firmly in his and without another word led the way to the patio. With luck, it was still unoccupied. If not, he'd find somewhere else. He meant to finish what he'd started.

Bridgette felt like a pull toy, being dragged in his wake. She hurried to keep up. "Where are we going?"

"Outside."

"Why?"

He didn't answer her until he'd closed the patio door behind him, and then it was with a question of his own. "Where's Roger?"

That again? "What?" Did he drag her out here just to grill her about a man who, because of him, no longer had any part of her life? Of all the pompous, egotistical—

She looked as if she were going to bolt. Blaine laid a hand on either shoulder, anchoring her in place. "You heard me, where's Roger? Why isn't he here?"

He just wasn't going to let this thing rest, was he? "Because we broke up. Satisfied?" she shouted at him.

"No, I'm not." His tone matched hers. Any minute, people were going to begin coming out, he thought. He didn't care. "Why?"

She threw her hands up. What did he want from her? Blood? "People do that. They break up."

That wasn't good enough. "I'm not interested in people, Bridgette, I'm interested in you, specifically." His eyes held hers. "Exclusively. Why did you break up?"

She pressed her lips together and looked up toward the sky, damning herself for feeling like crying. There wasn't anything to cry about. Was there? Yes, there was—her life was a mess. She'd given up a sure, stable life and risked her future because she'd fallen in love. And where had that gotten her? Shouting in her backyard.

Or what used to be her backyard, she amended, feeling the tears ready to brim.

She sniffed, hoping he didn't hear. "It wasn't fair to Roger."

Getting to his goal was like pulling teeth. "*What* wasn't fair to Roger?"

For two cents, she'd hit him. Maybe then she'd feel better.

"My going with him when I cared about another man." She lifted her chin pugnaciously as she glared at Blaine. "You want me to draw you a picture?"

She made a tempting target, he thought, struggling to control his temper. He didn't react well to being shouted at. "No, I want you to admit it, that's all. Admit that you care."

Was he deaf as well as insensitive? Boy, she could sure pick them. "I just *did*."

Not in so many words she hadn't. She'd taken a roundabout path. "Admit that you love me."

He'd like that, wouldn't he? To have her give up everything, hand him all the marbles, and then he could just walk off, smug. "Why should I admit that?"

She was the most stubborn, pigheaded woman in the world. And he couldn't live without her anymore. "Because it's true."

She'd had just about enough of his ego. "Look you—you face reader—"

He caught her extended palm in his hand just as she took a swing at him. "Because I love you."

She opened her mouth, but all that came out was a large rush of air. Bridgette stared at him, thunderstruck. Her hand dropped to her side as if it had suddenly turned to lead. "You love me?"

"Yes."

She couldn't believe it. There had to be a catch. "Is this a trick?"

Talk about suspicious. "If it is, I haven't learned it, yet."

She was having trouble getting air into her lungs. He loved her. She wouldn't have thought that of him. Desired her, yes, wanted her, sure. But loved?

Bridgette looked up into his eyes. Love. There was no missing it. "Wow."

He laughed as he began to take her into his arms. "That's exactly how I feel."

Love. He loved her. She hugged the word to her like a warm blanket. This made it all the harder to say no. "But I still can't move in with you."

Blaine didn't see the problem. He hadn't seen it all along. "Why not? Husbands and wives usually live together." A very sensual smile lifted the corners of his mouth. "It makes the evenings more interesting."

She'd stopped listening. Her mind was caught in first gear and plummeting down a hill. "Husbands and wives." Her mouth fell open. "At the risk of repeating myself—"

"You usually do."

She refused to be bated. This was too important. "Did I miss something?" When he began to lower his head to kiss her, she placed her hands on his chest, pushing him back. "When did you propose to me?"

He paused as if considering her question. "Probably from the first minute I met you. Officially, three minutes ago."

No, he hadn't. If he thought that was a proposal, he was sorely mistaken. She already knew her answer, had always known it, but she wanted him to do this right. "I didn't hear the words."

He tucked her against him. The fit was perfect. "You're supposed to be able to read my face, too."

She shook her head. Not good enough. "Words, Blaine. I want to hear words."

"Why?" he teased. "You say words all the time. What's a few more here or there?"

Her brow drew together threateningly. "Don't make me get ugly."

"Never happen. And I'm an expert on that." He stole one quick kiss and promised himself a second, richer installment shortly. "I love you, Bridgette Rafanelli, and I want you to marry me. To marry us," he amended, thinking of Mickey. "And I won't let you go back into the house until you say yes." The threat was accompanied by a smile that began in his eyes. "It's supposed to get really cold tonight."

She nestled into his arms. "I'm not worried. You could keep me warm."

He inclined his head, considering. "There's something to be said for that."

She turned her face up to his. "Yes."

"Yes, there's something to be said for that, or yes, you'll marry me?"

Bridgette felt as if a beam of sunshine had suddenly burst into her system. She could have hugged the world. She settled for hugging Blaine. "Yes, to everything."

He nodded. "About time," he agreed just before he kissed her.

* * * * *

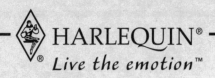

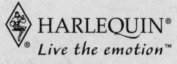

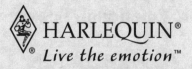

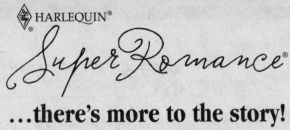
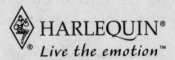

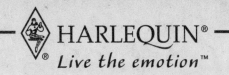